The Ghost of Lilly Pilly Creek
Abbie L. Martin

Book 1 - A Lilly Pilly Creek Ghost Mystery

THE GHOST OF LILLY PILLY CREEK

ISBN: 978-0-6457139-0-9
Abbie L. Martin Paperback edition / March 2023
Abbie L. Martin books are published by Abbie Allen Publishing

PROLOGUE

It had been two months since her sister died. Today Jones had decided she would finally return to The Memory Bank.

She was up early. No one else would be around to see Jones walk through the small Adelaide Hills town of Lilly Pilly Creek. All the residents knew she hadn't yet been back to The Memory Bank, to the site of Autumn's death. They had known her since she was a child, and had been patiently watching, waiting to see what she would do with the family business.

Jones had awoken abruptly that morning. She'd been dreaming of her perfectly normal life as a journalist. In the dream, she'd been getting ready for her workday, trying to dress whilst simultaneously rushing to arrange an interview for a breaking news story and texting photographers to meet her on location. Perfectly normal. Except the top she had pulled on in the dream was not one from her large t-shirt collection. No, when she turned to the mirror in her dream, the t-shirt Jones saw herself wearing, which would usually consist of a quirky slogan, was emblazoned with the logo of The Memory Bank. She'd been so shocked by this she had woken immediately and sat up in bed.

Jones had spent the past two months living in the home she grew up in, the home her sister Autumn had moved back into after their father's death three years ago. Returning to an empty house, with her parents and her sister all gone, had been hard. Yet, being back in Lilly Pilly Creek had also been somewhat comforting and familiar. She knew her grief was making it hard for her to return to Adelaide, to her

1

normal life, but there was a chance it was more than that.

So far Jones had managed to ignore the tugging questions of whether she was meant to continue her journalism career or take over the family business. She had assumed she would tidy things up at home, shut The Memory Bank for now, maybe rent out the building, and return to her thriving journalism career. Yet, here she was, still in Lilly Pilly Creek. This morning's dream appeared to challenge her to think about what she wanted. Was her future back in Adelaide, as a journalist, or was she meant to return permanently to her childhood home and continue The Memory Bank?

Jones realised the first step in making this decision was to actually step foot back in The Memory Bank. Preferably without the prying eyes of the townsfolk.

Now fully awake, Jones chose her Anne of Green Gables t-shirt which declared "Tomorrow is always fresh, with no mistakes in it." It seemed a fitting choice for the morning's task.

The walk would be less than fifteen minutes to The Memory Bank from the family home. The family home, where Jones and Autumn had grown up. Where their mother died when Jones was three and Autumn only one. Where their father had cared for them and created an amazing life, all on his own.

Jones pulled the house door closed and stepped out onto the brick pathway. It was crisp, as it often was in The Hills before the sun rose fully and warmed the town. Jones pulled her cardigan across her body and tucked her hands into her jeans. Closing the gate closed, Jones took in her childhood home for a moment, flashes of memories coming to her before she turned towards her destination.

The gorgeous old stone home was located on a street of equally old homes. Each one sat on a large quarter acre block, set back from the road, gardens filled with a mix of native Australian plants and English cottage flowers. This morning Jones delighted in walking past gum trees and rosemary bushes, grevillea and agapanthus. As the spring October days were warming, the colours of Lilly Pilly Creek seemed to pulse with purple, grey, light pink and green. Jones ran her hands through lavender flowers as she walked, before smelling the fragrance.

Sybil's coffee van was closed as Jones walked past. She realised how early it must be. Sybil was known for having her coffee machine pumping well before the other shops opened their doors. Today Sybil had her van parked near the playground. Jones smiled. It was the school holidays, so of course Sybil knew exactly where the coffee-demanding public would be positioned.

Timberley's Property & Real Estate was also closed, although the LED screens in the windows glowed brightly, displaying all the homes and commercial properties Prue Timberley had for sale or lease. Jones knew it would be Prue she would speak to when and if she decided to sell either The Memory Bank or the family home. Or both. The idea made her feel ill, but if it was required, Prue knew the local market better than anyone.

Jones heard some movement inside the Lilly Pilly Pantry. Part bakery, part providore, part grocery, part cafe, the Lilly Pilly Pantry was an Adelaide Hills establishment. The name may have changed over the years, but the shop itself had been a part of the town for as long as Jones could remember, and no doubt longer. She knew many people took Sunday drives to Lilly Pilly Creek just to visit the Pantry. Black and white umbrellas over timber tables lined the roadside. During sunny days every table was full of visitors drinking coffee and eating cheese platters or sourdough rolls with ham and chutney.

Just before she arrived at The Memory Bank Jones passed Hugo's. The wine bar was the newest venture in town, and Jones was yet to go inside. She had heard it was proving to be very popular, despite being a rather new concept for the town of Lilly Pilly Creek. Jones was pleased. She frequented wine bars regularly, living in Adelaide, and it was nice for a touch of the city to have come to the Adelaide Hills. As long as it was only a touch. She didn't want the country feel to diminish the town she had grown up in and loved.

Coming to a stop outside the tall wooden door of The Memory Bank, Jones paused. She was still unsure if she could face it. Still unsure that she would be able to walk through the door and return to the location of not only her sister's death, but a huge portion of her childhood.

Jones didn't know what to expect or why she had felt compelled to visit today. Secretly, she believed there might be some kind of answer for her in the walls of The Memory Bank. Perhaps she would be struck with an overwhelming feeling to quit her job and continue the family business. Perhaps she would realise that journalism was her destiny and it would be relatively easy to let go of her family's heritage after all. Perhaps the loss and emptiness she felt would be filled once she walked through that door.

Jones pulled a large key from her handbag. The key had been returned to her along with the other items Autumn had in her possession on the night she died. Jones hadn't taken anything else out of the bag, apart from the key, putting her hand in and rifling around until she gripped what she was looking for. Now, taking the cold, heavy key in her hand again, she pushed it into the lock. She hoped it would turn and that it hadn't seized up in the months since it had been opened.

Once, many years ago, The Memory Bank was originally a large and imposing bank building. In the seventies, her grandparents had bought it, not able to go past the opportunity to purchase such a building. Over the years the Eldershaw family had transformed it into a book store come stationery store come community hub. However, its most important feature was also the most unusual, and the pride and joy of the family.

Jones's grandmother had been passionate about family history and wanted somewhere safe to store all her treasures. It was her husband, Jones's grandfather, who had suggested using the old safety deposit boxes at the bank. At that time they were all empty and still with their original keys. Once the word got out about this wonderful idea, The Memory Bank was born. Customers wanted to store their items in the lockboxes as well. So the old bank building became a place for people to store their memories - diaries, papers, letters, photos - safely and securely. In a region that was prone to bushfires, one having arrived on the town's doorstep only a few years ago, this had proven to be a very popular service due to the thick, solid walls of the old bank. Now, all these years later, generations of families were still using the safety deposit boxes, and new people came in, requesting a box, regularly.

Jones smiled. The Memory Bank. A place dedicated to creating and storing memories. Where people could purchase a neighbour's memoir or book on local history, and then purchase the diary and notepaper they wanted to create their own. The Memory Bank took things full circle, by providing a place to store all of this for generations to come.

Jones was so proud of the legacy her family had created. Now, if only she could decide whether she would be the one to continue it. It took some effort, but the lock finally opened, signalled with a clunk. Jones was able to twist the large, brass handle and push the heavy door open.

The Memory Bank was always so dark when the first person entered. But Jones knew her way around, to the main light switch at least. She walked a short way, flicked the switch and waited. Jones loved this part. The bare bulbs scattered throughout the building turned on quickly, but it was the main attraction, the giant candelabra, that took its time to warm up. Jones walked slowly into The Bank, taking in the smells of the books, the paper, and cool stone walls, before stopping and staring as the candelabra flickered into life. For the first time in many months, she took a long deep breath and smiled. A genuine broad smile. It was familiar. So familiar that many happy memories suddenly flooded her mind, along with the emotions to go with each one.

Jones felt her throat catch for a moment before she shook her head and lowered her eyes. Now she looked upon the large circular counter that took up the centre of the room. The words 'The Memory Bank' shone in gorgeous brass letters on the front. It was the centrepiece of The Memory Bank. However, today there was something strikingly different about it.

"Oh my god!" Jones brought her hand to her mouth. She couldn't believe her eyes.

There, sitting on the top of the counter, long legs dangling beneath a bright red dress, was her sister Autumn.

"Hi Jones," she said, her voice calm and quiet.

Jones wobbled and suddenly found herself sitting on the ground, legs folded underneath her, heart pounding. Tears came to her eyes, blurring her vision. Jones blinked wildly, sure that her sister would disappear, and wondering what on earth had brought on this hallucination.

"Jones, it is me," said Autumn. "I'm really here, but if you want me to go away, just let me know."

"No!" gasped Jones. She rubbed her eyes, and pushed her hands into the ground, to ensure she stayed sitting. Then she looked up.

It was indeed her sister, sitting there on the counter. Autumn looked exactly like herself, except that she wasn't quite there. She was crystal clear, but also not completely solid. Jones could see the back wall behind Autumn. For a second Jones had allowed herself to believe that perhaps it had all been a dream. That Autumn hadn't died. She had just gone away for a while, and here she was, suddenly returned. Yet looking closer, Jones knew that wasn't the case.

Her sister had returned, she just wasn't alive.

CHAPTER 1

Today was the day. The Memory Bank was reopening! It had been six weeks since Autumn had appeared to Jones. In those six weeks, a lot had changed. Almost instantly Jones had decided she would take on the task of running The Memory Bank. How could she not, when her sister had come back! Jones had asked for a sign as she walked back into The Memory Bank, and boy had the universe delivered. Jones still wasn't sure if this was forever. Neither Jones nor Autumn had any clue how long Autumn, in her spectral form, would remain. But she was here for now, and Jones had to admit she was excited about the reopening today.

Jones's first port of call was Sybil's coffee van. It had now become her morning routine, after over a month of renovations in The Memory Bank. Sybil would look for her each morning, and Frank, Sybil's ginger cat, would most certainly ignore her.

"The usual please Sybil," said Jones. "But a double shot today. I think I'm going to need it!"

Jones's 'usual 'was a large flat white with full cream milk. But a stronger coffee was in order today. Jones stood quietly whilst Sybil, with her stone grey hair, today piled up high on her head, and wearing a flowing layered outfit of earthy colours, prepared coffee for the few customers patiently waiting beside her.

"The grand reopening," said Sybil. "The whole town's talking about it, aren't they Clancy!"

Jones turned to see who Sybil was talking to. It was a face she had not put eyes on for years.

"Good morning Jones," said Clancy. A somewhat shrivelled man looked at her. His white hair was a mess. He wore a knitted jumper with holes in it, fleece tracksuit pants, and what Jones could only describe as brown grandpa shoes. "Do you remember me?" he asked.

"Yes of course," Jones said, smiling. "You used to work for my Dad, didn't you?"

"I sure did," said Clancy, nodding as he leaned on his walking stick. "I'm pleased you've decided to keep The Bank open."

"Well, let's see how it goes," said Jones. It was day one after all and Jones didn't want to commit the rest of her life to The Memory Bank right then and there, especially to someone who had such a strong history with the place.

"Have a great day!" said Sybil, handing Jones a coffee, and slipping a surprise almond croissant into her hand.

"Oh, thank you, Sybil!" For some reason that small gesture made Jones's eyes fill with tears. She smiled at Sybil and quickly made her way from the van. "Nice to see you, Clancy," Jones called as she walked away. "Perhaps you'll come for a visit to The Memory Bank sometime time?"

Clancy waved and said, "I'll see what I can do."

Sipping her coffee, carefully as it was quite hot, Jones wondered for the millionth time if she was doing the right thing. She had taken leave from her reporter role at The Advertiser, Adelaide's largest print and online newspaper. It was initially only supposed to be a few weeks, maybe a month, while she grieved her sister's death. However, a few days after she had seen Autumn again, Jones had rung and said she would be taking leave without pay indefinitely and would get in touch once she 'had her life in order'. That way she still had an out if The Memory Bank reopening proved to be a failure. The newspaper had promised there would always be a job for her to go back to, but who knew how long that would last.

Jones was doing it for Autumn. She was doing it because all of a sudden, whether it was real or a hallucination, she had Autumn back, and there was no way she was letting that go without a fight. Yet, if Autumn disappeared one day, as Jones knew she would, would she still want The Memory Bank to be a part of her life?

Jones had always loved The Memory Bank, especially as a child. She would explore the back offices, and spend a lot of time up in what she called The Tower. The Tower was at the very top of The Bank. Its main function was to house and access the large clock that sat proudly atop The Memory Bank building. Years ago, to wind and maintain the clock, you would travel up the spiral stairs, although it hadn't worked for many years. The room behind the clock was tiny but big enough for a table, a couple of chairs, and a filing cabinet, a relic of the original Bank, which was now impossible to move back down the staircase. Jones had written many a story, drawn multiple art masterpieces, written numerous homework reports, or simply stared at the back of the clock, all from that Tower.

Autumn would sometimes have joined her, but mostly her sister was with their father. Autumn loved being with their Dad as much as she could, and especially loved learning everything about running the family business. The Memory Bank was always Autumn's destiny. Autumn was fantastic with the customers and was usually found in pride of place behind the circular counter. All their customers knew her, and as she got older, they would treat Autumn as an extension of their father, asking her questions, seeking her advice, and making many purchases with her.

There had been some envy on Jones's behalf. She often thought that if their mother was still alive, perhaps they would have been a pair, like Autumn and their father. In her teen years, Jones became very angry at the unfairness of losing her mother. She had been three when her mother died, and only had one strong memory of her. That memory, now bewildering in its foreshadowing, was of Jones and her mother in The Memory Bank's tower. The look of love and terror on her Mother's face when she had turned to find that her daughter had climbed up the Tower stairs by herself. The memory now made Jones shudder. The ache in her heart, knowing that it was at the bottom of the Tower's spiral staircase that Autumn was found, only a few months ago.

Jones arrived at The Memory Bank and took a moment to stand outside, staring up at the building. The facade extended up two storeys. A grand old bank, it had recently had its crisp white paint updated. Before it was The Memory Bank, Jones could visualise the raised letters of 'The Savings Bank of South Australia' being picked out in a strong black. Now, these letters too were painted white, but you could still see them at the top of the building, proudly displaying its heritage. 'The Memory Bank' was written in large gold lettering on the huge window to the left of the door. The writing was tastefully old-fashioned, and of an evening, when the lights were on inside, you could see rows of books, tables of journals, shelves of papers and pens, and much more through the glass. It was a glorious sight.

Pulling the key out of her handbag, Jones opened the large wooden door and entered.

Jones could smell fresh paint mixed with new books and the slight mustiness that all old buildings have. She sucked in a deep breath and exhaled loudly. In a sense she was breathing in the history and legacy of her family, hoping it would help her take on the day.

"Good morning!" Autumn almost sang the words as she twirled towards Jones. It was clear she was excited. Usually, Jones found Autumn, just as she had been that first day, perched on the counter, waiting. It was Autumn's preferred location, and often Jones had to shoo her out of the way. She could only imagine how inconvenient it would be when they had actual customers!

Today, however, Autumn was floating through the tables laid with all the gifts and stationery. Much of the renovations had been guided by Autumn. They were all the things she had been wanting to do for years but hadn't felt it was possible to close The Memory Bank for an update. The irony was, her own death was the perfect excuse.

Jones stared admiringly at her sister. She had noticed that although Autumn somehow managed to change her outfit most days (this being one of the ghostly abilities Autumn had discovered), she was always wearing something red, her favourite colour. Today, it was a red beret on her auburn hair, paired with red ballet flats, both in stark contrast to the black long-sleeve t-shirt and black capri pants she wore.

Jones joined Autumn in walking through the retail space, taking in all they had achieved, and ensuring it was all ship shape. They had added numerous antique timber tables to the furniture dotting the large room. The tables provided more space to lay out journals, books, pencils and bookish gifts. Jones had even added some candles, artwork and other items Autumn felt people would like to have decorating their home office or library. Jones had gotten into the habit of lighting one or two of the candles, creating a lovely atmosphere that she hoped the customers would notice.

However, Jones couldn't deny that she was nervous that the regulars might find the changes too much. Would they be worried that Autumn wouldn't have liked it? She didn't know how she was going to explain it and said this out loud to Autumn.

"Just tell them you found my journal where I'd written down all my ideas," said Autumn, floating over to Jones as she lit the first candle.

"Does such a journal exist?" asked Jones, placing the candle high up on a window sill and walking towards another collection of candles on top of a vintage card file, another item pulled in from one of the old bank rooms.

"Nope!" said Autumn, grinning. "I sell journals and buy plenty for myself, but never quite got into the actual task of journaling!"

"Sold," said Jones quietly.

"What?" asked Autumn.

"Oh, nothing," said Jones. It was tricky, judging whether to use past or present tense when it came to Autumn. She was dead, and yet still here.

Jones walked behind the counter and pulled out a bottle of cleaning spray and a cloth. She then started making her way around The Memory Bank, cleaning every surface in view, whether it needed it or not.

"So, what will I need to think about today?" asked Jones as she worked. "What if someone comes in wanting to access a lockbox? Or start a new one?"

Autumn shadowed Jones. As a ghost she was incapable of doing anything physically to help Jones get ready for today's reopening, so she could offer knowledge and advice instead.

"Well, if they want to access an existing box, you first have to make sure they have their key," said Autumn. "You then need to check the key number against the lockbox registry."

"The same registry that Atlas is currently adding to the computer, right?" Jones paused, holding a container of pens she had just lifted to wipe down the table, and smiled at Autumn.

Atlas Hemming had been brought in to help Jones prepare for the reopening. He was just meant to be an extra pair of hands around the place whilst they were renovating, but when he realised absolutely nothing of The Memory Bank's systems or records were on a computer, he made it his mission to get Jones up to speed. Jones was smiling because Atlas would constantly come out with exasperated remarks about how he couldn't believe Autumn hadn't digitised a thing.

"Seriously, she wasn't an old woman!" he'd mutter as he worked.

"Why make it so much harder?"

Autumn obviously couldn't respond to Atlas but would act affronted in a way that made it very clear to Jones that she wasn't impressed with his comments. Jones had considered revealing Autumn's existence to Atlas but she knew, as she was the only one who could see Autumn, he would simply think she was going delusional from grief. Jones herself still wasn't completely convinced that wasn't the case, but every day, when Autumn was still there waiting, she was more and more inclined to truly believe that Autumn had returned.

"Yes," sighed Autumn. "*That* register. But it isn't ready yet, so don't get too cocky. You're going to have to use the *actual* registers for a little while yet."

"Ok," said Jones with a grin. "So I check the register, for what?"

"You need to check that all their identification matches. They need to have three forms of identification, matching what you have on record, and there should also be a verbal password."

"Oh really! That's quite high security. People don't actually have anything valuable in there do they?"

"No, certainly no," said Autumn. "We don't allow valuables. We don't have insurance coverage for that. Or the security frankly. No, it is only supposed to be personal memorabilia-type information, family history, photos etcetera. But people do keep a lot of personal things in there too, diaries, letters, things they wouldn't necessarily want anyone else reading."

"What about fire?" asked Jones. "Do you worry that a bushfire could come through and destroy the building?

"That's why people prefer to use the old bank vaults. They're designed to withstand fire, up to a certain point at least," said Autumn. "That being said, we do recommend that people digitise everything as much as possible. When people buy a lockbox they sign a waiver that outlines all of this and more. I'll show you where they are later."

Jones finished up her cleaning and looked at the clock. It was nearing eight o'clock and Atlas was due to arrive at eight-thirty. He was going to help out on the floor while Jones was behind the counter. Atlas wasn't all that excited about suddenly becoming a retail assistant, but as he had said to Jones, he wouldn't miss reopening day for anything, so he'd pitch in wherever he was needed.

"Plus," said Atlas. "The money is proving to be very handy. I'm planning on buying a new computer to use for my side hustle." Atlas had then gone on to explain in detail the online platform he was creating, but most of it went over Jones's head. She was impressed just the same.

"So, we go and access the lockboxes with their key, after we've checked everything? And then we take them into one of the reading rooms?" Jones wanted to ensure she had covered as much as she could with Autumn before Atlas arrived. She moved behind the counter and was checking she had everything she needed, in particular, the lockbox registers.

"Yes, that's right. And they can't remove the lockbox from that room," said Autumn. "Just another added level of security. They need to pull the door locked on their way out and let us know they are leaving."

"Has this been learnt the hard way?" asked Jones.

"Oh I have lots of stories!" laughed Autumn. "But those are for another time. Perhaps over wine one night?"

"Over wine?" asked Jones. How on earth was Autumn going to drink a glass of wine?

"Well, you can have the wine," said Autumn. "But I'm going to pretend. I'm sure I'll at least be able to smell it. I still seem to be able to smell a lot of things, even if it is just in my imagination."

Jones smiled at this idea, picturing herself with Autumn at one of the cosy tables in Hugo's, sharing a bottle of wine. Just as it should be. Except there'd only be one glass.

Autumn and Jones walked through as many scenarios as they could think of in anticipation of the first customers. Jones felt completely inadequate and was relieved she was going to have Autumn by her side all day.

During the renovations, Jones had spent a lot of time debating with herself as to whether Autumn was there, a ghost, and not a figment of her imagination conjured up as a result of her grief. Jones knew logically it was impossible that Autumn was a ghost. And yet, there was so much depth to the experience, too much familiarity. Everything was exactly the same, the conversations, the way they spoke to each other, the way Autumn observed things. Autumn was also teaching Jones things about The Memory Bank that Jones couldn't possibly know. If Autumn wasn't really there, then how on earth was that happening? Because of this, because of the conversations and the knowledge Autumn was sharing with her, Jones couldn't help but conclude that Autumn was really back.

Yet, it wasn't exactly the same. Autumn couldn't touch Jones, they couldn't hug. Autumn couldn't touch anything without a mammoth effort. She could only really stay in The Memory Bank. It seemed The Memory Bank itself was what gave Autumn energy. They had tested the theory a few times and found, if Autumn somehow attached herself to Jones, and tapped into her energy, they could travel a little further afield. Yet this exhausted Jones and Autumn, so they were being very careful and taking things slowly.

When Jones thought about this all logically, it sounded ridiculous. The fact that she was having what she considered normal thoughts about whether Autumn could or could not travel out of The Memory Bank would no doubt sound crazy if she ever voiced them to another human being. For now, Jones was fully accepting and embracing the fact that Autumn was back, and was a ghost, without telling another soul. Without evidence to prove otherwise, it was the only real explanation for what was happening to her. Plus, it was wonderful to be able to spend all this time with her sister, even if she was dead.

Without Autumn, Jones had no idea how she would have gotten to this point. There was just so much about The Memory Bank she didn't know. Not for the first time, Jones wondered if that was why Autumn was still here, to help her with The Memory Bank and get it established. If this was the case, she wondered how long Autumn would stay. Would it all end sooner than either of them anticipated?

Just before eight thirty Atlas arrived. "Morning Jones, how are you feeling?" Atlas handed her another cup of Sybil's coffee.

"Oh thank you Atlas," said Jones, taking a quick gulp.

"I thought you could do with another coffee this morning," said Atlas.

Jones was completely unaware Atlas knew about her morning coffee routine and was impressed. He was a very observant person.

"You have no idea!" said Jones. "I'm feeling ok, just anxious to open the doors now."

"Well, let me get the computer going, and then we'll be ready," Atlas said. He moved behind the counter, pressed the power button, and logged in.

"Perhaps you should be the one behind the counter today?" suggested Jones. "I think processing sales might be a bit beyond me on that thing," she said, waving at the computer. "Maybe I'll be more use on the floor. What do you think?"

"I'm happy either way," said Atlas. "You know I'm always willing to take charge of the computer."

"Great!" said Jones.

She immediately felt more relaxed. Autumn was always the most sociable one of the two of them, but she felt much better talking with customers than worrying about making a mistake with the point-of-sale system Atlas had set up.

"Good idea," whispered Autumn. Jones jumped.

"Shh," said Jones. "Please don't do that to me!"

Autumn pealed with laughter. "Oh Jones, you were always so easy to scare!"

"We're going to have to come up with some kind of system," Jones hissed. "If I jump like that too often people are going to think I'm going mad!"

At that moment there was a loud knock on the door. It was two minutes to nine but obviously, someone was eager for the grand reopening to begin.

"Well," said Jones. "Here we go!"

"Whoop!" called out Atlas from the counter, pushing up his glasses, with a wide grin on his face.

Autumn joined in with the whooping, as Jones made her way to the door.

CHAPTER 2

Jones couldn't help but smile as she pulled open the big wooden doors. There, standing on the other side was someone holding a giant vase of flowers.

"Congratulations!" Wren cried. "Happy reopening day!"

Jones almost burst into tears. She took the vase from her friend Wren and turned quickly to put them on one of the tables, hoping Wren didn't notice her trying to hide her face.

"Thank you! Wow, these are amazing!" Jones felt her voice quiver and was sure Wren, and Autumn, could hear it.

Jones had gone all the way through primary and high school with Wren. They'd kept in touch during their University years and their first years in the working world, even though they had moved in different circles at that time. After Wren opened up her law practice in their hometown, and Jones was working the crazy hours of a journalist in the city, they hadn't seen each other very often. Now they were both back in Lilly Pilly Creek, it was just like always. Not only that, Wren had been a real lifeline for Jones over the last few months.

A few of Jones's newspaper colleagues had texted or rung to check in and see how she was. It was nice that they did genuinely seem concerned about her. Many of them had started together at the newspaper as cadets, before moving into their specialised roles. After-work drinks, consoling each other on missed stories or applauding each other when they landed a front page brought them even closer together. It was the city family she needed, the family who got what the journalist's life was all about. Yet, it wasn't her true family, the ones she'd always had waiting for her in Lilly Pilly Creek. Now, she had the ghostly Autumn, and her longest friend in the world, Wren.

Wren wove throughout the tables, picking up books, peering at the paper shelf, and running her hand along the antique table tops. Wren was wearing a classically tailored suit, a style that she was known for. A charcoal grey jacket and trousers and a high-necked blouse in mustard yellow, with earrings to match. She looked amazing. Wren sniffed one of the candles with a smile, and then stood in the middle of the room and spun around, her black curls bouncing around her face.

"Look at this place! Oh, you've done a wonderful job, Jones," Wren said, beaming at her friend. "It looks the same but different. It's perfect."

"We're really happy," said Jones, and then realised her mistake. We. She had meant she and Autumn. Fortunately, she realised Wren just assumed she had included Atlas, so no awkward glance came her way. Jones felt her chest tighten a little as she realised how nice it had been to have Autumn to herself for the last few weeks. Jones could only imagine how hard it was going to be to pretend she wasn't around when the customers arrived. She just hoped no one would notice or would blame her grief.

"Now Jones," said Wren, walking up to her friend. "I've also got something to tell you."

"Oh yes?" Jones turned from where she was straightening a line of perfectly straight books. She had noted the tone of her friend's voice and knew she had something serious to discuss.

"Jamie's back," said Wren. Wren watched Jones's face closely, clearly trying to read her expression at this news.

"Jamie Jamie?" asked Jones. She was surprised to hear this news but equally surprised to find she had no strong feelings either way.

"Yes, Jamie, Autumn's-boyfriend-who-hasn't-been-seen-since-the-funeral Jamie."

Jones heard Autumn make a shocked sort of sound and desperately tried to ignore her.

Jones didn't know what to think. No one knew why Jamie Royce, Autumn's boyfriend, had left immediately after the funeral. Jones had just assumed it was all too overwhelming for him. In the lead-up to the funeral, he'd been a huge support to Jones. Jamie had helped her with anything she'd asked of him, and one night they'd shared a bottle of wine, and cried and laughed together as they told stories about Autumn. However, the day after the funeral, when she'd popped around to his house to drop off something, his housemate had told her Jamie had left for the city early that morning and they didn't know when he'd get back. Jones assumed he'd touch base with her, but he never did, despite the few calls and text messages she'd made. Jones realised he had ghosted her, and the irony as she remembered this now, didn't go unnoticed.

Jones wasn't particularly concerned. They'd never really been close and certainly weren't in each other's lives before Autumn died. Jamie and Autumn had only been dating for about six months before her death, which meant Jones and Jamie had only caught up a couple of times. Yet, she had still been a little surprised when he had simply left and not contacted her. They seemed to share a bond, being one of the few people who had had a close relationship with her sister. Perhaps it was just all too hard for him. He needed to separate himself from that part of his life. Jones completely understood this.

With Autumn floating around the room, Jones wasn't sure what to say next. She tried to subtly look for Autumn to see what her expression was, but Autumn had, most likely intentionally, gone out of her eye line.

"Do you know why he's back?" Jones asked, hoping it was an appropriately inconsequential question.

"Well, apparently he's had some big business success, and is looking at investing back into the community."

"Really?" said Jones. "Well that sounds interesting I suppose."

"It must be so hard for him," said Wren. "Losing his girlfriend after such a short time together. It's not like they were getting married or anything. Well, not that I know of. It's like he doesn't have an official position in her life, now that she's not here any more. I wonder if that's why he's doing it. Why he's back to invest? To somehow still be a part of Autumn's life?"

"Yes maybe," said Jones, and then, because she couldn't help herself, "although I'm still here. I'm a connection to Autumn. He could have chosen to speak with me, instead of ignoring me."

Wren shrugged her shoulders and was clearly about to say something else, but The Memory Bank's main door was suddenly and violently opened. A very tall woman with a sharp bob and short skirt was storming across The Bank's timber floors, her black high heels ricocheting loudly.

"Jones!" the woman called, her arm waving. "Jones! I must speak with you!"

"Here we go," said Wren under her breath.

The woman striding towards them was Prue Timberley of Timberley Real Estate. Prue had a reputation for being very community minded but also a very shrewd and relentless businesswoman. It was widely known that she was buying up a lot of the local buildings, and it had been made clear to Jones by much of the population over the previous weeks, that The Memory Bank was high on her list of potential acquisitions. Jones had ignored a few letters she'd received from Prue recently, but today was apparently the day they were finally going to speak in person. Whether Jones liked it or not.

"Oh Jones," said Prue, taking a cursory glance around The Memory Bank. "Well, this all looks wonderful. Wonderful. Now," Prue stopped, folded her arms across her chest, and tipped her hip, attempting a pleasant smile. "Jones, I've been desperate to speak to you. I hope now is a good time?"

"Hello Prue," said Jones, attempting her own pleasant smile, which she was sure looked more like a hyena's grin. "Thanks for popping in for our grand reopening," Jones said this a little too loudly, recognising a bit of spitefulness in herself. It was unusual for her, but she noticed she was feeling quite protective of The Memory Bank, and perhaps this was a defence mechanism.

"Well, of course," said Prue "It's a big day for you I realise. I only hope it is a success. However….”

Jones couldn’t resist raising her eyebrows. What on earth was Prue going to say?

“However, is it really something you want to be taking on? In your time of such deep, deep grief,” said Prue, frowning and bending her head to the side. “I mean you are doing *so* well with your journalism. I’ve followed your career you know.” Jones doubted that was true. “The Memory Bank was Autumn’s little project. Carrying on from your father. It’s not really you, is it?”

“How dare she!” Jones heard Autumn from across the room. Jones lifted her chin and rolled her shoulders back.

“I don’t know what you mean Prue. I mean, it is *my* Bank now.”

“Yes, yes, I know you *own* it. But is it the best path for you?” Prue spread her arms wide, looking up and around the room. “Isn’t it going to limit you? Limit your career? I mean Lilly Pilly Creek isn’t exactly known for its thriving media industry, is it?” Prue attempted a laugh, but she wasn’t trying to be funny.

“Well, I don’t know Prue. You know Lilly Pilly Creek isn’t as small as it seems. I don’t consider being in Lilly Pilly Creek to be career-limiting at all.” Jones felt Wren stiffen a little next to her, deliberately leaning into her friend. Jones appreciated the communication of moral support.

“Oh no, no, of course not!” said Prue, clasping her hands in from of her chest. “Not at all, not at all. It’s wonderful for the right people, for those who are ready to focus long-term on the community.” Prue looked directly into Jones’s eyes as she said this. “But is that what you plan to do? Is that your dream? Why not consider selling The Memory Bank to someone who can guarantee its future? And you can get back to your city career."

"Oh Prue, honestly!" said Wren, unable to keep her mouth shut any longer. Jones looked at her friend, smiling and shook her head slightly, indicating she could handle things. Wren nodded and turned back to Prue.

"Prue," said Jones, crossing her arms. "As you would be aware, my sister only died two months ago. Therefore, I am simply not in the frame of mind to discuss this. If, *when*, I am ready, I will reach out to you. In the meantime, I would prefer if you left me alone."

Prue pursed her lips, looking closely at Jones. She nodded and reached out her hand to Jones. Jones thought this was a little ridiculous, but shook the hand she was offered.

"Thank you, Jones," said Prue. "I am very sorry for your loss. Autumn was a wonderful person and it is lovely you have taken on The Memory Bank for her. I know she too would only want what's best. For the whole community."

Jones heard Autumn scoffing in the background. Jones couldn't believe that Prue allowed herself one final jibe. But then, that was just the type of person she was.

Prue took herself and her loud high heels out of The Bank.

"That woman is a piece of work!" said Wren, her hands on her hips. "How dare she walk in here like that, and just as you were opening the doors for the first time."

"I'm sure she doesn't mean any harm," said Jones, rubbing her forehead, trying to relieve some tension. "She just doesn't have great communication skills."

"Oh she knows exactly what she's doing!" said Wren, turning to face Jones. "You know- oh, never mind. Not the right time." Wren turned away and ran her hands down her thighs, appearing to be simultaneously straightening her trousers and releasing some tension.

"What?" asked Jones, walking around to face her friend. "Come on Wren, you know you'll tell me eventually."

"No Jones," Wren shook her head. "this is your big reopening, I don't want to ruin it."

"What do you mean? What could ruin it?" Jones's eyebrows moved together sharply.

"Look Jones, it's probably not that big a deal anyway. It's just," Wren looked down at her hands, and then made sure she was looking Jones in the eye as she continued. "You just shouldn't trust her. She's only out for herself and, well, the thing is," Wren paused, glancing at the ceiling for a moment, before bringing her eyes back to Jones. "Look, a lot of things have been said about Prue and her connection to Autumn. What I'm trying to say is, some people thought that Prue had something to do with Autumn's death. Her murder."

"Murder!" Autumn cried, at the same time Jones rapidly drew her head back, crying out "what?" That was a word she hadn't heard in connection to her sister's death. "Her murder? You think Prue, *murdered* Autumn?"

Autumn had rapidly made her way to Jones's side, waiting to hear what Wren would say.

"Jones I'm sorry, I'm sorry. I shouldn't have said anything." Wren took her friend's hands and squeezed them. "Of course, it was going to upset you. And on the grand reopening. I'm so sorry." Wren went to hug Jones, but Jones put her hand up, stopping her friend.

"No, it's fine. It's fine. I'm not upset," said Jones, gripping Wren's shoulders. "But you need to tell me what you know. Autumn wasn't murdered. It was an accident. The police said so. Right?" Jones took a step back, looking closely at her friend, seeking answers.

"Yes Jones," said Wren, clasping her own hands, clearly not knowing what to do with them. "And I'm sure that's all correct. It was only a rumour. Town gossip. You know how it is. I shouldn't have mentioned it.

"Ask her what else she knows. Who told her this?" hissed Autumn.

"Do you know anything else?" asked Jones.

"No, not that I can think of," said Wren. "It was just a group of us talking at the bar one night. We probably had a bit too much to drink, and a few people were talking about who would have a reason to want Autumn dead. It just seemed that a lot of people's first thought was Prue. That's all."

"Ok," said Jones. "Well, I suppose that is just speculation. Autumn probably wasn't murdered, and Prue surely couldn't do something like that." Yet even as she said it, Jones felt silly for never considering that Autumn's death was perhaps more than an accident. Maybe it was a possibility. Perhaps the police had missed something.

Wren walked over to one of the tables and picked up the handbag she had left there. "But I still wouldn't trust Prue," she said, hooking the bag over her elbow and facing Jones. "Be very careful around her. She's trying to buy up the whole town and from what we've just seen, it seems she'll stop at nothing, not even a recent death, to get what she wants."

Wren could no longer hold back and reached out, hugging her friend. Jones almost didn't know what to do, but then relented and relaxed into the hug. Jones could feel her eyes beginning to brim with tears. Things were suddenly feeling rather overwhelming. The morning of the grand opening, of all days, it's suddenly revealed Autumn may have been murdered. It would be enough for anyone to fall in a heap. But not Jones.

"Are you ok?" asked Wren.

"Of course I am Wren," said Jones. "Please don't be worried. I'm glad you said something. I haven't been home for so long, I don't know what's been happening and all the local politics. I'll make sure I'm very careful around Prue." Jones felt her hands shaking a little as she released herself from Wren's hug.

"Look I have to go," said Wren. "But shall we catch up for drinks tonight? At Hugo's? When you close. To celebrate."

It took a moment for Jones to respond. It wasn't until Autumn hissed "say yes!" in her ear that she finally answered Wren's questions.

"Yes," Jones smiled. "Yes, that sounds like a great idea. Perfect. I'll meet you there at say six?"

"Excellent!" said Wren. She appeared to have relaxed a little. Jones didn't want Wren to worry about her. She was fine, and she had a big day to focus on.

"Thanks for the flowers!" Jones called after her friend.

"Of course!" Wren waved as she walked towards the door. "Have a great day! I can't wait to hear all about it at Hugo's!"

Jones smiled and waved. Then, shaking her head, she took a moment to regroup and look around her. Customers had arrived but she hadn't noticed. She rolled her shoulders back, lifted her chin and put a smile on her face. It was the grand reopening after all, and she had work to do! Even if she had just discovered Autumn may have been murdered.

CHAPTER 3

The reopening was a huge success. Jones was sure the locals had made a point of coming in to support her that day as it was busier than anyone could have anticipated. Atlas was scanning products almost nonstop. There was only a slight lull in the middle of the afternoon when Jones was able to sit down for a moment and grab a bite to eat.

As soon as Wren had left that morning, Autumn had started hovering around Jones, trying to get her attention. It was of course obvious that Autumn wanted to talk about Wren's revelation. Jones did too. Her mind was racing at a million miles an hour. Having Autumn flittering around as well was not helping Jones focus on the customers in front of her. Just before eleven Jones managed to catch Autumn in a quiet spot.

"Autumn, I know we need to talk about this, but I'm too busy!" Jones whispered, quickly glancing around hoping no one was observing her talking to herself in the corner.

"I know Jones, but come on, this is crazy news," Autumn's hands were on her head as if trying to force her ghost brain to make sense of it all.

"Yes, crazy is a word," said Jones. "And if I'm seen talking to myself, every customer out there is going to think *I'm* crazy."

"Ok, ok, I'll wait until you have a quiet moment," said Autumn, and the two of them turned to cast their eyes across the shop floor filled with customers. "Surely the novelty of the grand reopening will wear off soon." The two of them looked at each other and grinned.

The novelty did not wear off.

When she locked the doors at five o'clock that afternoon, Jones couldn't take the smile off her face.

Turning she saw Autumn reclining on one of the now-empty sofas, beaming and raising her arms in triumphant support for her sister.

"Atlas, that was insane!" Jones said as she walked to the counter and slumped into a stool next to him.

Atlas was smiling too but didn't look up from the computer.

"Mental!" he said. "Look at how many sales we made!" Atlas spun the computer monitor towards Jones so she could take a look.

"Wow!" said Jones, doing her best to interpret the rows and rows of numbers on the screen. All she saw was the dollar figure at the bottom of the table, and she was flabbergasted.

Autumn had come up behind her and was looking too. "Amazing! I never had a day of sales like this, ever."

Jones glanced towards her sister, knowing Atlas was engrossed in the numbers on the screen. She beamed and then spoke to both of them. "I simply can't believe it. I mean, it was probably just because it was the opening day. It won't be like this again, but what a great start."

"I heard a lot of good things," said Atlas, finally taking his hands off the keyboard and turning to face Jones. "So many people were saying how proud Autumn would have been, and that they knew she would be happy with all the changes you've made. I think more people will be back than you think."

"Too right!" said Autumn so loudly Jones was sure Atlas must have heard. If he had, he made no sign, instead turning back to the computer and continuing to tap away.

"Did anyone open any new lockboxes today?" Atlas asked as he worked.

"No," said Jones. "There were a few who wanted to add some more items to their boxes, which I think I handled ok," said Jones, shrugging a question at her sister, who nodded eagerly. "But today it seems everyone was interested in the stationery and books and gifts. Maybe they didn't want to bother us too much on the first day. Thank goodness! I don't think I would have remembered what to do."

Jones was quite glad she didn't have to handle too many of the lockboxes today. It was so busy she had been worried she would make a mistake on one of them, open the wrong lockbox or forget the security steps.

"You know I would have helped you," said Autumn. Jones looked at her and smiled. Despite the two of them being desperate for a quiet moment to speak, Autumn had been a tremendous help to Jones all day. Without Autumn by her side, reminding her of things, commenting as needed, and in general, calming her down, Jones wasn't sure she would have made it through the day.

"Well, I might just print off some reports for you, if that's ok?" said Atlas.

"That would be great," said Jones. "I'm going to leave just before six if you'll be ready by then?"

"Easy done," said Atlas.

Autumn was vigorously waving at Jones, motioning her away from the desk. Jones pretended to wander through the tables, checking on things and adjusting anything that was out of place.

"Jones," said Autumn. "We need to talk. Away from Atlas. Shall we go up to the tower?"

The tower? Jones was surprised by Autumn's suggestion. She understood why Autumn had chosen that location. It was the furthest away from the front counter, which meant Jones could talk to Autumn normally without Atlas hearing. Yet, was Autumn willing to take Jones back to the scene of her death? Possibly her murder?

Jones had understandably thought about Wren's suggestion multiple times that day. However, she had managed to push the thought away as quickly as it came. The idea that her sister had been murdered instead of simply falling down the stairs was too big a concept for her to consider whilst she had been smiling and chatting to customers. Yet, now that the shop was closed, and she would soon be heading over to Hugo's with Wren, she knew she had to speak with her sister.

"Couldn't we go into the lockbox vault?" asked Jones. The thought of walking up those stairs made her feel a little ill. So far she had managed to completely avoid it.

"No, I want to go to the Tower.," Autumn insisted. "I think it's the best place."

Jones wanted to argue, but it was difficult to argue with a ghost in front of other people. She was sure Autumn had thought of this. Jones nodded and followed her sister.

Jones tried to hide her puffing at the top of the spiral staircase, and held onto the bannister for a moment, before walking into the Tower.

She realised her fitness probably wasn't quite where it should be. Autumn of course was fine. Apparently, ghosts didn't feel the tug in their calf muscles or the catch in their lungs after walking up a steep staircase. When Jones finally managed to lumber into the Tower room, Autumn was there waiting, standing at the large mechanism of the clock, the face of which looked out to the street below.

"What do you think?" Autumn asked.

"About climbing a hundred stairs after the longest day on my feet ever. Not impressed!" Jones knew what Autumn had meant but needed to catch her breath, leaning her back against the cool plaster wall.

"Ha ha," said Autumn. "I mean, what do you think about Wren saying I was murdered?"

"It sounds ridiculous," said Jones, as she took a seat at the small table in the back of the room. "The police said it was an accident. I'm sure they wouldn't have lied."

"Well who knows," said Autumn. "Perhaps they didn't lie. Perhaps they did think it was an accident. But did they ever actually investigate anything? Do you know?"

"I don't think so," said Jones. "At least not seriously if they had. I don't recall murder ever being mentioned. It was always considered an accident right from the start as far as I know. And your autopsy seemed to prove it."

"I had an autopsy?" Autumn raised her eyebrows in disbelief.

"Well yes, of course," said Jones, surprised that this was the thing that seemed to shock her sister.

"Why would they give me an autopsy if they thought it was an accident? Why would they cut up this gorgeous specimen?" Autumn said, sliding her hands down her body to reinforce how gorgeous her sister already knew she was.

Jones couldn't help but laugh at that, before responding to Autumn's question. "I don't know. I thought it was just routine. No one was there when you died, so I think they have to."

"Well, Wren has certainly got me thinking about *other* possibilities," said Autumn, who had started to pace back and forth in front of the clock, as though she were its pendulum.

"What? You think Prue murdered you?" Jones was still coming to grips with the idea of her sister being murdered. To think that the awful woman who had strode into The Memory Bank that morning, asking Jones to sell this very building to her, was the one to push Autumn down the stairs. Well, she realised it wasn't completely out of the realm of possibility, but the idea made her shudder.

"Not Prue," said Autumn "I mean maybe. But no, what I mean is, perhaps I *was* murdered by someone. It's worthing considering, isn't it? I just wish I could remember that night. Why can't I?" Autumn turned to look at her sister, and for the first time, Jones saw some real sorrow on Autumn's face. It was long after Autumn appeared that the two of them had spoken of her death. Jones had asked her several times what she remembered, and Autumn always told her that she couldn't remember anything about the days leading up to her death, or her actual death.

"I'm sure there is some scientific explanation," said Jones. Then, realising this sounded a little ridiculous, continued jokingly. "You know, the extensive and rigorous scientific research that's been done into why ghosts can't remember their deaths. In fact, why don't we google it now!"

Both Jones and Autumn had to laugh. The two of them appeared to be taking Autumn's ghostly presence in their stride, but the unlikeliness of the situation struck them both on the oddest occasions.

"Autumn," asked Jones. "You still don't remember anything at all of that night?"

"No," said Autumn. "Absolutely nothing. I mean, I hadn't tried all that hard before today. I didn't think it was something I truly wanted to remember. But since Wren told you that people thought Prue had murdered me, I've been trying to wrack my brains all day. That's why I wanted to come up here."

"It is?" Jones frowned. She for one couldn't imagine wanting to return to the location of your death. Then again, she also couldn't imagine dying and returning as a ghost.

"Yes, I thought being here again might spark a memory," said Autumn. "But all I'm thinking about is how much time you used to spend up here as a kid. You were always up here, weren't you?"

"Yes I was," said Jones. "It was my own, quiet space." She turned around to take a proper look at the tower room. Jones ran her hand over the wooden table she has spent so many hours at, reading, studying, and writing. It had always been her treasured place. Now it had become a place of great sadness.

"Jones!" They heard a voice from downstairs. It was Atlas. "Jones, can you hear me?"

"Yes, Atlas! I can hear you!" Jones had almost forgotten Atlas was down there. She moved to the top of the staircase, but couldn't see him from that angle.

"Well I'm heading off!" he called up to her. "I've left the reports on the counter!"

"Thanks, Atlas!" Jones yelled back. "You were amazing today!"

Jones knew she should quickly race down and thank Atlas properly, but she didn't think she could physically do it. She would never race down those stairs again, not like she did as a teenager.

"No worries! See you tomorrow." Jones heard Atlas pull the door closed.

Jones turned to Autumn and managed a smile. "Do you think we did ok?"

She genuinely wanted the opinion of her sister. The sister who should be the one physically enjoying this moment, relishing in all she had accomplished. Instead, it was Jones. Jones, who knew so little about The Memory Bank. Jones, who had always planned to leave Lilly Pilly Creek. Jones, who was now back, living the life Autumn was meant to have.

"Jones." Autumn walked up to her and tried to stroke Jones's face, before frowning. Autumn looked at her sister again and smiled. "Jones, it was amazing. There was nothing more you could have done. It was just like I had always imagined, but only you were able to pull it off."

"Oh Autumn," said Jones. "You would have done this too, eventually. You know you would." Jones felt her heart tighten, the ache of grief, which had dispersed a little since Autumn's incorporeal return, pounding again.

"I'm not so sure," said Autumn. "At least, not without your help. Thank you."

Jones felt her eyes begin to water. She stared at her sister a little longer and then said "Well, shall we go down and finish up for the day?"

"Absolutely!" Autumn beamed. "And then, a drink!"

Jones laughed and began to make her way, slowly, down the stairs.

CHAPTER 4

"I wonder what Dad would think?" said Autumn following Jones down the spiral staircase.

"About the reopening?" said Jones. "I think he would have been amazed. Amazed that I was the one running the show, for starters. Well, kind of running the show."

"Jones," said Autumn. "He would have thought it was bloody brilliant!"

The pair laughed. He wasn't the most demonstrative father. The sisters always knew he was proud of them, but showed it in his unique way. For example, when Jones got her first job and told her Dad she was thinking about buying a particular car, he drove to Adelaide without telling her and spent the day visiting car yards, before calling her to tell her he had found a car for her. She had absolutely no idea he was doing this, and she was very relieved that her Dad had taken all the work out of her hands.

Autumn floated in front of Jones as she finished her descent. "No, what I meant was, what do you think Dad would have thought about my death?"

"Oh Autumn," Jones said, sadness showing in her eyes. All this talk of Autumn's death, something the two of them had managed to somehow avoid for most of the time they'd been renovating The Memory Bank, was bringing up so many emotions for her.

"I don't mean, would he have been sad. I know he would have been," said Autumn. "No, I mean, do you think he would have thought it was an accident? Would he have thought I was murdered? Would he have made the police investigate?"

"You mean you think *I* should have made them investigate?" Jones said, slightly louder than she meant, pursing her lips. She was surprised her sister would say such a thing.

"No!" said Autumn. "No! Of course not." Autumn's face showed shock, and she waved her hands quickly in front of her, as though trying to erase what she had just said. "The thought hadn't crossed either of our minds, Jones. Of course, I don't think you should have asked them to investigate. The police told you it was an accident. Why would you think anything else?"

Jones kept her eyes down as Autumn spoke, being somewhat more thorough in organising her handbag than she normally was.

"Jones, I was just wondering. You know how Dad was. He never really trusted authority, did he?" Autumn was attempting to grip the end of the counter but wasn't having any luck, so she shook her hands as though trying to release her emotions through them. "Dad always seemed to have hunches about people. I just wonder if he was here, what his hunch might be right now? Would he think it possible that Prue could have killed me?"

"Or maybe it was someone else," said Jones. "Maybe someone else killed you." Autumn winced at this comment, still clearly uncomfortable with the idea that someone, anyone, may have taken her life. However, Jones had just realised, if Prue could be considered a murderer by some people, simply because she wanted to take The Memory Bank away from Autumn, then perhaps they needed to consider the fact that someone did want to kill Autumn.

"Autumn, this morning I was still thinking your death was an accident. I don't have a good reason to genuinely think it was anything other than an accident," said Jones, slinging her handbag over her shoulder and walking from behind the counter. "But if we're going to seriously consider that your death was a murder, then we also need to seriously consider who could have done it. And I mean all possibilities."

"Not Prue?"Autumn walked next to Jones as she went around blowing out candles, checking doors were locked, and turning off lights.

"I have no idea about Prue," said Jones. "Wren seems to think it's possible. But why? Is she the type of person who would kill just for a building?"

"It seems unlikely. Although she is rather, ah, passionate," said Autumn.

"That's an understatement," Jones rolled her eyes as she bent to blow out a group of candles next to drawers of parchment.

"But if not her, then who?" Autumn was running her hand up and down her opposite arm. It was a gesture Jones recognised, one Autumn did subconsciously when she was trying to calm herself, almost as though she was hugging herself.

"I have absolutely no idea," said Jones. "But I'd better lock up. I'm meant to be meeting Wren in twenty minutes."

"We," said Autumn. "We're meeting Wren?"

"We are?" asked Jones. "Can you go as far as Hugo's?"

"I'm damn well going to try. It's my celebration too." Autumn smiled at her sister. Champagne was one of Autumn's favourite things in the world. Death wasn't going to stop her from celebrating with a glass of bubbles.

Jones continued to make her way around the tables, straightening up things, noting areas she was going to have to top up in the morning. Nearly all the Moleskin notebooks had been sold. The packs of Pentel Energel journalling pens were also popular, as were the Japanese Zebra two-tone highlighters. Jones was pleased to see some of the candles had been sold too, many of which had been supplied by a local candle maker.

As she worked tidying the counter and putting everything away, Jones wondered what her Dad would have thought of the addition of gifts to the mix of paper-related products. She thought he would approve. After all, it was her parents who introduced the paper and notebooks to The Memory Bank, the store her grandfather and grandmother had opened in the seventies.

Originally The Memory Bank was opened as a place for creating and storing memories. Her grandfather hadn't been able to go past the opportunity to purchase the bank building when it came on the market. Although, according to their father, he had no idea what he was going to do with it. To start with their grandfather had hired out the various rooms for offices and the larger areas for community meetings and workshops. It was her grandmother's idea to start using the lockboxes that had been the real hit, and gradually they began selling local history books and family memoirs, the start of the retail side of The Memory Bank.

Her grandparents had retired not long after Jones and Autumn's parents had married, and the young couple had taken over The Memory Bank. Their father loved The Bank and did his best to live up to his parent's legacy. He encouraged a real community feel in The Bank, hosting many events, occasionally having artwork on display, inviting guest speakers, as well as a variety of other events. Their Mother, a lover of books and writing, having studied European Literature at University, had encouraged the expansion of more books and the introduction of paper products into The Memory Bank.

Tragically their mother had died when Autumn and Jones were very little. Breast cancer. "Taken way too quickly and way too young" their Dad always said. He spoke of her often, but Jones couldn't remember her mother. Occasionally there was a smell that seemed to float past, bringing her mother to mind. However, it was their Dad who was the centre of their world, and thus, The Memory Bank. Both girls loved The Bank, although in different ways. Jones loved the quiet spaces she could find and was often found reading or writing in one of the old bank storage rooms or the Clock Tower. Autumn would be following her Dad around, helping him with chores, and eventually serving customers. It wasn't surprising that instead of going to University, Autumn decided to work with her father, with the vision of taking over The Memory Bank one day. It had unfortunately occurred a lot earlier than either girl expected.

Their father had died of a heart attack in his fifties. He'd collapsed in The Memory Bank just after closing time. It had been Autumn who had found him, returning after spending the day in the city at a retail expo. No, Autumn's was not the first dead body to be found in The Memory Bank, although the autopsy had made it certain there wasn't anything suspicious about *his* death.

Autumn was devastated obviously, but in loyalty to their father, she barely closed the shop for more than a few days. They even had the funeral on a Sunday when the shop would have been closed anyway. Autumn loved her father so much, she was adamant she was going to carry on, no matter what. Jones had tried to get Autumn to take a break, but she was busy, with her journalism career just starting to take off. They had mourned their father. Yet, both had to get on with their lives. Sometimes Jones wondered if it was the right thing to do. Especially now that Autumn had died. Although thankfully, for now, she was not gone.

"Jones, do you think we have time to have a quick look in the ledgers?" asked Autumn as Jones finished straightening one of the last shelves.

"Why?" asked Jones.

"I thought if I perhaps looked at the most recent entries, you know, before I died, it might shine some light on any issues I was having. Because for the life of me, I can't remember anything."

"For the life of you?" Jones raised her eyebrows.

"You know what I mean!" They both laughed. "Whatever the alternative phrase of 'for the life of me' is for a ghost!"

"Well, quickly," Jones said, glancing at her watch "Where do we start?"

Autumn took Jones down into the basement. It was lit by only a few naked bulbs and was very cool. The basement was one of the places Jones came to as a child, especially when it was scorching hot outside and she was looking for a refuge from the heat, as well as from the bustle of the main Bank area.

"A perfect spot for a wine cellar!" Jones said out loud as she wandered around, waiting for Autumn to find what she was looking for.

"Oh tell me about it!" said Autumn. "But Dad never did agree with me."

Autumn called Jones over to one of the filing cabinets and had her sister pull out some large leather books. Inside was thick parchment paper, with dates, notes and numbers of all sorts.

"This is the cabinet Atlas has been working on," said Autumn. "But I don't think he's gotten to these front ones yet."

Jones flicked through trying to find the most recent one. As she did, she noticed a familiar name.

"Clancy!" said Jones. "That's a coincidence. I ran into him this morning. He used to work here, right?"

"Yep, that's right," said Autumn. "He used to work for Dad when we were younger."

"Yes, I kind of remember," said Jones. "I knew he worked for Dad but I don't remember seeing him in The Bank."

"What's it say about Clancy?" asked Autumn.

"Oh, nothing that I can see. It's just his name and a time next to it. Maybe you were meeting him or something?"

"Yeah, maybe," said Autumn.

Jones flipped through another ledger and finally found the most recent one, the one with Autumn's handwriting on the pages.

"Yes, that's it," said Autumn. "But it will have to wait. It's six o'clock."

Jones looked at her watch. Autumn was right. She carried the heavy tome back up the stairs and slid it into a drawer in the main counter, which she promptly locked. "Let's try and have a look tomorrow. I'm assuming we won't be quite as busy. But first, wine."

"To Hugo's!" Autumn cried, holding her arm out in front of her as if she was Maria in The Sound of Music, leading the children over the hills.

CHAPTER 5

As they locked up and walked to Hugo's Wine Bar next door, Jones kept anxiously glancing at Autumn, wondering if she would suddenly disappear as they got further away from The Memory Bank. Jones decided conversation was the best distraction.

"How come you can remember Clancy working at The Bank, how to run The Bank and so many other things," asked Jones. "But you can't remember anything about your death?"

"I have absolutely no idea," said Autumn, wrapping her translucent arm around Jones's, even though neither of them could feel it. "I wish I did. It is so frustrating. It's like that entire day is lost to me. That entire week or so. This would all be a whole lot easier if I could actually remember dying and the days leading up to it. I wonder if other ghosts remember their deaths?"

Jones paused at the door of Hugo's and turned to her sister.

"Do you think there are other ghosts?" she asked, quietly.

Autumn shrugged. "There have to be, surely!"

Jones reached out for the handle of Hugo's black door and paused. It was a gorgeous painted timber door with a glass window of retro reeded glass, the kind you would have found in pubs everywhere in the seventies and eighties. The windows on either side were open and Jones listened to the happy sounds of customers inside. She needed to remind herself that to everyone in there, it would appear that she was walking in alone.

"Go in, go in," pestered Autumn. Jones gripped the large brass knob and turned.

Hugo's was busy, with people dotted throughout the space. They either sat at marble-topped tables on black bentwood chairs, were lined up on stools at the bar, or perched at the open servery windows along the front and side.

Behind the bar, pouring wine, and shaking cocktails was the man himself, Hugo.

Jones hadn't officially met Hugo yet. She had seen him around, and he had been pointed out, the way anyone new to the town was pointed out to a local like Jones. Hugo had travelled the world, she'd been told, America, Europe, and Asia, and had decided to bring the quaint wine bar culture back to South Australia. For some reason, Lilly Pilly Creek was identified as the perfect location for his venture. Jones was surprised her little hometown had been the choice, but as she looked around, she was impressed and pleased.

"Jones!" There was Wren, at the bar, waving at Jones to join her. Wren's dark curls framed her face as she beamed at Jones.

"Here we go," murmured Jones so only Autumn heard.

"Don't forget to buy me some champagne," Autumn said.

Jones walked up to Wren who gave her a giant hug. Wren was very much a hug type of person, unlike Jones. "The champagne is on me!" said Wren. "I heard your day was a great success."

"You did?" Jones looked surprised, wondering if the whole town was talking about her.

"Your protégée over there told me," said Wren, pointing to a table in the corner. It was taken up with a group of young men, all in front of laptops, drinking beers, talking animatedly, barely taking their eyes off their screens. One of those young men was Atlas. He seemed to sense them because at that moment he was the only one to lift his eyes and spot them staring at him. He smiled, waved, and then returned to his computer.

"Well, it was a pretty good day," said Jones. "And Atlas was brilliant." She was pleased that he had enjoyed the day so much that he was telling others about it. "Although I'm not sure I'd call him my protégée. I don't think I've taught him a thing. This computer stuff is all him. Plus, I can't see him hanging around long. Once the system is set up and I kind of know what I'm doing, I'm sure he'll be bored and off to the next thing."

"I wouldn't be so sure about that," said Wren, perching herself up on a stool. "He was pretty enthusiastic when I spoke to him."

Jones smiled, and glanced at him again, realising that she barely knew a thing about Atlas, except that he was a lot younger than her and a whiz with computers.

"Ah, here's Hugo!" said Wren. "Hugo! Come and meet the lady of the hour!"

Jones, realising Wren was talking about her, felt her cheeks burn. She was not one for attention, usually keeping behind the scenes. It was why she preferred print media to television or radio when it came to her journalism. She could spend most of her time behind a phone or a computer.

Walking towards them was Hugo. He was a tall man, with a beard that Jones wasn't sure was just a few days of stubble growth, or intentionally manicured to be that way. His dark brown hair was wavy but not too long, and he wore black jeans and an olive green and brown check shirt. Hugo smiled at both of them, flipping a tea towel over his shoulder, and propping himself up with his hands on the bar.

"Wren, what can I do for you?" Hugo smiled broadly. He clearly knew Wren well. Jones was surprised this was the first time she had met him, but then she realised she hadn't been in much of a state to meet anyone over the last few months.

"Well, drinks of course! But first, please, meet my friend Jones. Jones, meet Hugo." Wren rested her hand on Jones's shoulder.

Jones smiled. "Hi, Hugo, nice to meet you.'

"Is this *the* Jones?" he asked, reaching his hand out. Jones felt her cheeks go even redder, which wasn't helped when she heard Autumn whisper *"The* Jones?" Jones went to swat her sister away and then remembered that was pointless. Fortunately, she could hide it by taking Hugo's hand and shaking it.

"It sure is!" said Wren. *"The* Jones of *The* Memory Bank and my wonderful friend. Who, might I say, has just had the most amazing reopening day."

"Oh really?" said Hugo, looking into Jones's eyes just long enough to make her feel even more awkward and glance away. "Well, that sounds like a cause for celebration!"

"Champagne please Hugo. The real stuff!" said Wren. Jones was getting the impression that Wren was a regular at Hugo's. She looked at the relaxed way they spoke to each other and wondered if they were perhaps more than friends.

"Coming right up! I can bring it to your table if you like. Where are you sitting?" Hugo walked to the fridge behind him and rested his hand on the handle whilst waiting for Wren's answer.

"Oh, we'll head outside I think Hugo. Near the fairy lights!" Wren picked up her bag and pointed outside to show Jones the way to head.

"Not a problem. I'll grab it now," he smiled and went to move off.

"Oh Hugo?" said Jones, before Hugo could go far. Hugo turned back to Jones and tilted his head. "Would you be able to take something over to Atlas please?" Jones asked. "Do you happen to know what he likes to drink? He deserves a celebration too. He did most of the work today."

"Absolutely!" agreed Hugo. "I happen to know he is partial to scotch and coke. What do you think?"

"Sounds perfect! If you could get that from me, I would really appreciate it."

"Will do! I'll add it to the tab." With that Hugo strode away.

Wren gripped Jones's arm and said "So, what do you think?

"What do I think of what?" Jones looked around the room, ready to tell Wren how impressed she was with the bar.

"Hugo of course. Isn't he gorgeous!"

Jones turned to Wren, trying to get a read. "He seems lovely. Are you two, you know-?" Jones shrugged her shoulders at Wren.

"What? Oh no!" Wren laughed! "You know I'm not really into guys."

"You had plenty of boyfriends at university?" Jones was a little confused.

"And girlfriends if you recall," Wren raised her eyebrows with a smile. "University was just experimenting. Nope, I've completely moved on from that phase. It's girls for me one hundred per cent now. I just have to find the right one!"

Jones smiled, and happily followed Wren to the rear of the bar. She couldn't exactly explain why she was feeling so particularly pleased that Wren wasn't into Hugo. Jones pushed that thought out of her head as she admired the garden area they had just walked into.

"Wow," she said, letting out a long breath.

"Isn't it amazing," said Wren. "Hugo has done a brilliant job."

Large white light bulbs were lit above them, strung from the timber pergola that crisscrossed overhead. The pergola was covered in wisteria, which in the middle of October, was still covered in its glorious purple floral bunches. The pristine green lawn was bordered by gravel and pot plants of all shapes and sizes. Groups stood at wine barrels, reclined on large cushions on the lawn, or sat at various tables dotted around. The air was warm, and Jones could catch the sound of Lilly Pilly Creek itself, flowing behind them, beyond the huge gum trees lining its banks.

Fortunately, there were still a few tables available on the gravel edge. They sat down on metal chairs, and before long Hugo arrived with an ice bucket, the champagne bottle, and two crystal glasses. One of his staff was also by his side, putting a cheese platter on the table.

"On the house," Hugo smiled at them. "Congratulations Jones, on continuing your sister's legacy. The whole town is thrilled The Memory Bank is open again. Thank you." Hugo looked deep into her eyes, and Jones almost forgot to breathe. She was taken aback by his words. A stranger who was so invested in The Memory Bank. Perhaps The Bank did mean almost as much to the town as it did to her and Autumn.

"Thank you, Hugo," Jones said quietly. He held her gaze for a moment longer, smiled, and then turned to pour the champagne.

Once he was finished, Hugo replaced the bottle in the ice bucket. "Enjoy!" he said and walked back into the bar.

Wren was watching Jones, a grin on her face, but she said nothing. Instead, she handed one of the glasses to Jones and said "To The Memory Bank!" Jones repeated her words and they clinked glasses. Autumn was hovering near one of the poles holding up the fairy lights. She was swaying and appearing to bask in the atmosphere. Jones managed to catch Autumn's eye, tilted the glass her way, and they smiled.

"So, was it amazing?" asked Wren. "Did you really, truly have a great day?"

"Look I couldn't have asked for more," said Jones. "No major dramas, everyone seemed happy, and according to Atlas, we had brilliant sales. So day one, I can confidently say was a success. I'm just not sure about day two and beyond." Jones sipped her champagne, thrilling in the tiny bubbles that coated her tongue. If only her sister could taste this. Autumn had requested champagne, but Jones had no idea how she could deliver on that promise.

"Oh, you'll be fantastic Jones! You are perfect for this." Wren clasped her friend's hands, as though wanting to force her enthusiasm into Jones.

"Do you think so?" asked Jones. "I mean, The Bank was much more Autumn's thing. And Dad's."

"Of course, they were amazing. Autumn just loved The Memory Bank and everyone loved her," said Wren, sipping her wine. "But I think you are going to bring something even more to The Bank, to the town."

"Woah," said Jones. "Let's not set expectations too high. I mean I'm not even sure if I'm cut out for this in the long term." Jones looked down at the table and held in her next sentence for a moment before saying, "Perhaps Prue is right? Perhaps it would be better in someone else's hands?" She quickly glanced at Wren and then back at her own hands, wrapped around the crystal stem of her champagne glass. Jones knew Autumn had heard her, yet she didn't dare turn to view the expression on her face. Instead, Jones tried to picture herself at the helm of The Memory Bank for many years to come. She just wasn't sure.

"Look Jones," said Wren. "I know journalism is what you love. And I know you also love The Memory Bank. I have this feeling that you're going to find a way to combine the two. I think something special just might happen if you're patient."

Jones looked up at Wren, trying to read her face and work out what she meant.

"Wren, you are sounding very wise tonight," smiled Jones.

Wren playfully flicked her hair behind her ear and struck a pose. "Oh, you haven't seen anything!" Wren laughed, and gulped her wine, realising her glass was already empty.

As Wren poured more champagne into both their glasses, Jones just had to ask, "Wren, do you really think Autumn could have been," she hesitated, and moved her head closer to Wren's, speaking quietly. "Murdered?" Jones sensed Autumn had walked up close behind her. She must have heard the question.

Wren looked quickly around and then leaned into Jones. "Of course, I don't have any real evidence, but I do think it's something you should consider. Call it a feeling. Call it a hunch based on rumours I've heard. But I think the police think so too, they just have nothing to prove it, so they're calling it an accident unless they find out something more."

"But I thought the case was closed?" Jones was genuinely confused, wondering how Wren seemed to know so much.

"Look Jones, I don't have any inside information or anything," said Wren, attempting to answer the question Jones was trying to pose. "But if I were you, I'd think about going and asking the police. They might know more than they've told you so far."

Jones sat back and stared at Wren. She was a little stunned. Yes, she and Autumn had only just been talking about the possibility of Autumn's death being murder, but Jones realised she hadn't believed it. Yet, the way Wren was talking made her feel sick in her stomach. Who on earth would want Autumn dead?

Jones didn't have time to ponder this question any further.

"Warning at nine o'clock," Wren said softly. "It's Jamie, and he's coming our way."

CHAPTER 6

This was the last thing Jones wanted. She was not mentally prepared for a conversation with Jamie. She didn't want to get sucked back into the grief they had shared up until Autumn's funeral. Having Autumn around her, she had been able to escape that feeling. Jamie didn't have that same fortune, however, and Jones wasn't sure she could cope with his inevitable despair. Jones looked quickly up at Autumn, and she was surprised to see an unpleasant look on her face. Autumn was staring at Jamie as he crossed the lawn to Jones and Wren's table.

When Jones turned to look at Jamie, it was not exactly what she was expecting. He strode across the lawn, holding a drink in his hand as if he owned the place. He was smiling broadly, waving and greeting various people, and appearing to be having the best day of his life. It was nothing like Jamie had been when Jones last saw him.

"Jones!' Jamie cried. "Jones!" He strode up to the table and lifted Jones out of her seat. "How are you? How are you feeling?" Jamie held Jones at arm's length, taking her in, before wrapping her into an enveloping hug. Jones was stunned. She awkwardly patted him on the back, before he finally released her.

"Hello Jamie," Jones said, furrowing her brow. "You seem... happy?"

"Oh Jones," said Jamie. "I'm sorry, I wasn't thinking. It's wrong of me to be celebrating when you must still be grieving." He looked over at Wren and spotted the champagne on their table. "Oh, but are you celebrating too?" he asked, returning to look at Jones.

"It was the reopening of The Memory Bank today," explained Jones. "It was a good day, so Wren has bought us a bottle of champagne."

"Of course," Jamie said, smacking himself on the forehead. "How stupid of me. Of course, I had heard today was the reopening. Sorry, I've just been absorbed in a few business deals I've got happening. Big things, all go go, but that's no excuse. Jones, I'm pleased for you. Well done. Although," he peered at her. "I didn't think you were going to take over The Bank. I thought you were thinking of selling it."

"Well," said Jones. "No decisions have been made. You did leave right after Autumn's funeral. It's taken me a while just to get things straight in my head. But I think it's the right move, for now at least."

"Absolutely!" said Jamie. "Well, would you mind if I pulled up a pew and joined you?"

Jones looked at Wren, who appeared to be holding back an eye roll. Instead, Wren nodded her head and said "Of course Jamie. Grab a seat."

Jamie made his way to a table nearby and asked them if he could use an empty chair, before returning with it to sit with them.

"So Jones," Jamie said, taking her hands in his and staring at her. "How are you really?"

Jones was surprised at how awkward this felt. In those weeks leading up to Autumn's funeral, they had seemed to get close, just like brother and sister-in-law. They had listened to each other, held each other up, and taken turns managing everything, when the other needed to fall in a heap.

Now, with Jamie sitting in front of her, things seemed different. Perhaps it was because he had left so suddenly after the funeral and hadn't been in contact since. Perhaps the inevitable distance was already between them, now that there wasn't anything to hold them together. Or perhaps it was because Jones knew Autumn was right there, watching them. Yes, that must be it.

Jones resisted the temptation to flick her eyes to Autumn, and instead replied to Jamie.

"I'm good Jamie. As good as can be expected." Jones managed to pull her hands away, feigning the need to take another sip of champagne. "The Bank has been a great distraction, and to be honest, I'm pleased to be able to keep it open. I feel a stronger connection to Autumn and my Dad when I'm there." Little did anyone know quite how strong the connection with Autumn was.

"I'm so pleased," said Jamie. He leaned back in his chair and ran his hand through his greying brown hair. "So, what were you two chatting about before I walked up?"

Wren looked at Jones, who shrugged her shoulders. Why shouldn't Jamie know about their hunch? He had been Autumn's boyfriend, after all. Jones noticed Autumn out of the corner of her eye. She was moving closer, looking directly at Jamie. Autumn didn't say anything, but it appeared clear she was waiting for one of them to mention the possibility that her death hadn't been an accident.

"Well, actually Jamie," said Wren. "We'd quite like to know your thoughts on something."

Jamie beamed, pleased they were seeking his advice. He clasped his hands together, and placed them on the table, appearing ready to espouse his wisdom.

"Jamie," said Jones, leaning in a little. "Did anyone ever mention anything to you about Autumn's death possibly being....ah....murder?"

Jamie's face went immediately pale. His mouth dropped open and he pushed himself back from the table.

"What? Murder? What?" Jamie didn't seem to be able to form a complete sentence. Jones realised the idea of Autumn being murdered was as much of a shock to Jamie as it had been to her earlier that same day.

"I know Jamie, we've always been told Autumn's death was an accident," said Jones. "It's just, well, Wren mentioned something today and now I just can't seem to shake it."

"Mentioned something?" Jamie took a long sip of his drink before turning to Wren. "What did you mention, Wren?

"You need to keep this quiet Jamie," said Wren, leaning in a little closer. "It's just a rumour. I know nothing, and Jones is going to speak to the police, so you can't say anything to anyone."

Jamie leaned in, looking at Wren, and nodded his head. "Absolutely. It's just between us."

"I had heard some rumours that the police had considered the fact that Autumn's death may not have been an accident," Wren told him. "Then people started mentioning one person in particular, who had something to gain from Autumn's death."

"Oh yes? And who would that be?" Jamie asked.

"Prue Timberley," whispered Wren.

"Prue!" Jamie said a little louder than they were all comfortable with. "Sorry, sorry," he said, bringing his volume back down. "Prue? Seriously? Why on earth would she want to kill Autumn?"

"For The Bank of course!" said Wren.

Jones looked sternly at Wren who was getting a little loud herself.

"It's just if it wasn't an accident. Prue does seem rather desperate to get The Memory Bank," said Jones, talking at an appropriately low level. "She's been sending me letters constantly, and today, on the day of the reopening, she was in The Bank offering to buy it again. I would have thought she'd at least let me enjoy the reopening. But no, there she was, first thing, implying that I wasn't the right person to take over The Bank and that I'd be stupid not to sell to her." Jones looked at Wren who raised her eyebrows. "Well, perhaps not in those exact words, but that was the implication."

"I wouldn't have thought Prue would have the balls to do something like that," said Jamie. "I guess you do never know though. She does sound overly keen to get her hands on The Bank. However, if I had to pick anyone who might want Autumn dead," he glanced around before leaning even further over the table, "and honestly, even saying that is hard, well I'd pick Clancy."

Jones saw Autumn's head wrench backwards and she knew she was just as surprised as Jones to hear that name again so quickly.

"Clancy?" Jones tilted her head and furrowed her brow. "I didn't realise you knew Clancy. Why do you think he might be involved?"

Did Jamie even really know Clancy? Jamie wasn't a long-term resident of Lilly Pilly Creek. He had lived there for a few years before meeting Autumn, but he wasn't known to be a huge part of the community. At least that was Jones's understanding.

"Well, didn't he used to work at The Memory Bank?" said Jamie.

"Yes," said Jones. "But it was a very long time ago. I'm not quite sure how that could be relevant?"

"It might not be," said Jamie. "But I do know that he wasn't on good terms after they left. Autumn told me. I think we had a conversation about him quite soon before Autumn's death." Autumn had walked behind Jamie so Jones could see her. "I remember we were on a date at a winery, I think it was Pike and Joyce, and we had a bit of a discussion about it. I can't remember." Autumn shrugged her shoulders, making it clear she couldn't remember. "I think at the time I was too busy trying to sort out an issue with one of my investment properties so I was a little distracted." He put his hands to his temples and closed his eyes, as though forcing something from his memory. "It's just, I seem to recall that Clancy had been in touch with Autumn again. Something had happened. I just don't remember what it was."

"Well, I was going to have a chat with Clancy anyway," said Jones. "Thought he might have some insights on running The Bank, so I might try and find out what it was all about."

"That certainly sounds like it might be worth it," said Jamie, as he stood up from his chair. "Well, great to see you both. I'll make sure I pop into The Memory Bank soon." He smiled at them both before turning to Jones. "Please be careful. If someone did kill Autumn, then it means they're still out there." He squeezed her shoulders and turned away.

She watched him as he left. Jones found herself feeling a little guilty for springing such shocking news on him, especially when it had been so long since she had seen him. And he had been in such good spirits. Hopefully, he'd be ok.

Jones looked up to see Autumn pacing between the fairy light poles. It was time to go.

"Wren, I'm sorry," said Jones. "I think I need to leave." Like a veteran actress, Jones let out a yawn to full effect.

"Of course, of course," said Wren. "It's been a big day. The reopening, and dredging up all this stuff about Autumn's death. You must be wiped."

Wren pulled the champagne bottle out of the ice bucket and emptied the remainder into her glass. "You go. I'll just sit at the bar and chat with Hugo while I finish this. Unless you wanted me to walk you home?"

Jones realised Jamie's words had freaked Wren out a little too.

"No, no," said Jones, looking at Autumn who was clearly desperate to speak with her. Wren's presence would not be helpful. "I'll be totally fine. It's no different to any other night."

"Well, text me when you get home," said Wren. "You know, just to be safe."

Jones hugged Wren, thanking her for the drinks and the chat, and all of her support. Wren swatted her away but grinned all the same. Jones left her chatting with Hugo. Hugo waved goodbye and as she waved back, Jones wondered what that strange feeling was in her chest.

CHAPTER 7

Autumn was pacing the sidewalk in front of Hugo's when Jones walked out the door.

"It's quite strange," said Autumn. "but as soon as I saw Jamie I got such a sad and frustrated feeling. I had the overwhelming sense that we were broken up."

"What?" Jones said, surprised at the intensity in Autumn's voice. Jones instinctively went to put her arm around Autumn and guide her back to The Memory Bank. Of course, her arm when straight through her sister, which was a little horrifying, but fortunately, Autumn recognised what Jones was trying to do, and started walking.

"I just have the impression that we'd broken up before I died. It's almost like a memory is trying to come back. Do you remember?" Autumn turned to look at Jones. "Had we broken up?"

Autumn couldn't keep still, hovering back and forth in front of Jones as she walked. Jones kept feeling like she was going to bump into Autumn, but realised that was impossible. However, there was no way she wanted to literally walk through her sister, so she kept pausing and trying to dodge her. Things were weird enough as it was.

"It's not anything I ever heard," said Jones. "And Jamie certainly didn't mention it after you died. I think perhaps you've got your wires crossed on this one. Maybe your memory is missing for more than just a day or so before your death. Perhaps it's a bit fuzzy in general? But what about Clancy? Do you remember anything about being angry with him?"

"Nope, nothing. But you could be right, maybe my memory is just unreliable," said Autumn. "And to be honest, I'm not feeling the best right now either. It's taken a lot of energy for me to be at Hugo's with you tonight. I think I need to get back to The Bank. Hopefully, my connection there gives me some strength."

"Oh Autumn!" said Jones, the colour in her face draining away in panic. "I'm sorry. I should have realised. Do you want me to stay with you? I can sleep on one of the couches?"

"No! I'll be fine," said Autumn. "I can feel myself improving the closer we get to The Bank. I'm still learning what this ghost stuff is all about, but I think for some reason I get my energy, my life force if you can say that, from The Bank. It makes sense I guess. Being as that's where I died."

"And where you used a lot of your energy *before* you died," said Jones. "The Memory Bank was the place that energised you the most."

Autumn smiled. She liked that idea.

"Well, good night Jones," Autumn said as they reached the door. Instinctively, Jones reached into her purse for her key. "No need to unlock the door, Jones!" Autumn laughed. "I'll see you bright and early for the beginning of the rest!" Autumn slid through the door and out of sight.

Jones pondered her sister's words as she walked away from The Memory Bank towards home, not quite sure how to interpret the phrase, 'the beginning of the rest'. Was The Memory Bank the beginning of the rest? The rest of her life? Is that what Autumn had meant?

Jones's mind flicked back to Wren's comments about combining The Memory Bank and her journalism career. The concept sparked a little something in Jones, but she couldn't think of any way that it might work. Jones wondered if Wren had some ideas for her. Could she create a *new* life that included everything important to her?

Yet, how could Jones possibly think about her own life, when the whole day had been hijacked by talk of Autumn's death? Or more accurately, her murder.

Could Wren be right, was her sister murdered? And if so, by whom? Prue was obsessed with The Memory Bank but obsessed enough to kill? Perhaps. And Clancy. Why did Jamie think he would have a reason to kill Autumn? It seemed a bizarre idea, considering he hadn't had anything to do with the family or The Memory Bank for years. At least as far as Jones knew. Was Jamie remembering the conversation he had with Autumn correctly? Were she and Clancy really on bad terms? Autumn's memory couldn't be relied upon, so there was certainly a possibility Clancy could be connected. Jones knew she would have to investigate Clancy further.

Amongst all this contemplation of her sister's possible murder, Jones couldn't help finding her thoughts flicking to Hugo. Why? He seemed like a nice person, and Wren was certainly close with him. But they'd only just met. Jones wasn't really in the right frame of mind to consider a relationship with anyone, let alone someone who lived and worked in the same town, the town she wasn't even sure if she was going to stay in long term.

As Jones turned onto her tree-lined street and walked under one of the street lights, all she could see in front of her was her past. This was the road she had learnt to ride a bike on. It was the street her father had driven home not one but two new cars when they were kids. It was the road she walked every day to and from primary school, and then to and from the bus stop for high school. She had held Autumn's hand as they walked to the playground, and when they were old enough to go and buy ice creams by themselves at the petrol station around the corner. And it was the street she would drive down as she headed off to Adelaide and the little flat she shared with friends when she was at University. It was the road she had driven when she left this town. And it was the road she had driven early that morning when she had rushed back after Autumn's death. Rushing to an empty house.

Was the house she grew up in meant to become her home again? She supposed it would always be her home, but would it be her forever home, to live in, to stay in? She had no idea, and right now, as she pushed the wire garden gate open, and made her way inside the house, she was simply too tired to think about it any more.

Jones automatically reached to switch the light on, and the long hallway with its timber floors and the well-worn runner was lit up. The walls were lined with artwork and bookshelves, and on the floor there were piles of various items. It was a sight she had seen her whole life. To her left was the formal living and to the right her father's bedroom. She continued down where her bedroom was to the left and her sister's to the right. The bathroom was next on the right, opposite a small study used by her father. Jones opened the door at the end of the hallway into the large kitchen, which had been opened up and extended when she was a teenager. Jones flipped the lights on over the kitchen island and poured herself a glass of water, before quickly texting Wren to let her know she'd arrived home safely.

She realised the cheese platter Hugo had so kindly given them, hadn't quite filled her up. In the fridge, she found some of last night's Thai green curry, one of her favourite meals to cook, which she zapped in the microwave. Perching herself on a stool at the kitchen island, she devoured the curry and fragrant jasmine rice, a glass of sparkling mineral water next to her. She sat and listened to the peace. The tick of the kitchen clock, and the hum of the refrigerator. A dog barked in the distance, and a breeze rustled the golden elm in the garden.

An overwhelming feeling of home hit her as she sat there. Even without her father and sister, this house, this town, was undoubtedly her home. It was something she simply couldn't let go of. She had never imagined living in Lilly Pilly Creek as an adult. Yet, she had always believed her childhood home would be here whenever she needed it because her father and then her sister would always be here. Now things had changed, she simply couldn't imagine no longer having this home. Her breath caught in her throat, and she found herself crying over her curry. It wasn't fair. It wasn't fair that she was the only one in her family left. It wasn't fair that her mother died so young, and now her sister had followed in her footsteps. It wasn't fair that her father was no longer here to guide her, to help her make the decisions she needed to make.

Then she remembered who was there. Jones realised how thankful she was for Wren, who had assumed the role of supporter and champion ever since Autumn's funeral. Before that, if she was honest with herself. Jones realised she perhaps hadn't noticed how much help Wren had been, because she was too busy with Jamie as they enveloped each other in their grief. She remembered that whilst she and Jamie sat at the dining table she was now staring at, Wren was in the background making them food, cleaning, putting them to bed, and making sure both of them were where they needed to be. Jones suddenly felt immense guilt for taking her friend so much for granted. Now she realised she hadn't thanked Wren properly for everything she had done. Too preoccupied with Autumn and The Memory Bank, pretending things between the sisters were almost back to normal.

It seemed Jones now had two people to thank tomorrow. She wouldn't take Atlas or Wren for granted anymore. For now though, it was time for bed.

CHAPTER 8

Jones arrived at Sybil's for her usual coffee and was relieved there was no sign of Clancy. She wasn't sure if she wouldn't act uncomfortable around him, or, worse still, ask him an awkward question. Just because Jamie referred to him as a potential murder suspect didn't mean he actually was. Yet, Jones still knew she couldn't trust herself to act normal today.

Sybil chatted away as she poured the double shot Jones had once again asked for. Today Sybil wore her grey hair long over a pair of denim overalls. Underneath she wore a yellow and purple abstract shirt, the sleeves rolled up to her elbows.

"Everyone is very impressed," Sybil said. "I hear you've done a lovely job with The Bank. I'm hoping I'll get a chance to pop in soon."

"That's nice to hear," said Jones. "It was certainly busier than I expected."

"I also heard you had a particularly interesting visitor?" Sybil said, not taking her eyes off the milk she is frothing.

"Oh? Which visitor would that be?" A lot had happened in the last twenty-four hours. The grand reopening and the discovery that Autumn may have been murdered meant she had a lot on her mind.

"Ms Take-Over-the-World herself, Prue Timberley of course." Sybil looked up at Jones and smiled. "You're not thinking of actually selling to her, are you?"

"Ah, that's who you're talking about," Jones realised she'd almost forgotten about Prue's proposition. "I suppose I shouldn't be surprised how fast news travels around here." Jones rolled her eyes with a smirk as Sybil handed her the takeaway cup. "And no, at this stage I'm not thinking of selling. I barely even know what I'm doing *today*. I can't think any further than that."

"Look Jones, if you are thinking of selling, and I'm not saying I think you should. Not at all," said Sybil. "But, if you do, just don't automatically offer The Memory Bank to Prue. She rubs a lot of people the wrong way, and perhaps others might like the opportunity." Sybil had her hands planted firmly on the coffee van counter and looked intensely at Jones.

"What do you mean, she rubs people the wrong way?" asked Jones. Wren's words from yesterday were ringing in her ears. Prue was a prickly person, but beyond that, if there was information that could connect her to Autumn's death, then Jones wanted to hear it.

"It's like she's on a mission to buy up the whole town. She says she's only doing it for the community, to ensure Lilly Pilly Creek stays true to its roots, and that she's the only one willing to do it. Pfft!" Sybil rolled her eyes. "But she puts a lot of pressure on people, and doesn't seem to be against seeking out people when they're at their most vulnerable," said Sybil, staring pointedly at Jones. "All I'm saying is, make sure whatever you decide to do is on your terms. Take your time. I know many people in this town would love for you to stay, myself included." Sybil ended her rant with her arms crossed over her chest and a smile on her face.

Jones was touched by Sybil's words. She was never quite sure how accepted she was by the community. Yes, she was considered a local.

But she never knew if people *liked* her. She knew everyone loved her sister and her father. She even knew how much everyone loved her mother and her grandparents because people had told her many times over the years. Yet, she didn't quite know how she fit into the town. Maybe, just maybe, she was a part of this town after all.

When Jones arrived at The Memory Bank, Autumn, today wearing a red trench coat over jeans and boots, was waiting for her on the side of the table closest to the door.

"Well that's a nice t-shirt choice today," said Autumn.

Jones frowned and looked down, forgetting what she had chosen.

'What would Lorelai do?' She almost laughed. It was her Gilmore Girls top and Autumn was right.

"Well, what *would* Lorelai do?" she asked Autumn, flicking on the main light switch.

"No idea. But you've made a good start with the coffee."

Jones couldn't help but grin, realising that Lorelai would visit Luke's every morning for coffee, just like she visited Sybil.

"What I think we should do first is take a visit to the police station," said Autumn in a firm tone.

"Well yes, I think we should too. But why are you feeling so strongly about it today?" Jones peered at her sister. Autumn had been waiting for her at the front door and had certainly gotten right to the point this morning.

"It's a feeling I have, I mean a real feeling," said Autumn, following Jones to the counter. "I don't know if it's from being a ghost, but after seeing Jamie last night, I realised I'm getting quite a different sense of people these days. Being around Jamie, I am sure things weren't as happy as he has made out. If we weren't broken up, I think we were on the verge of it. So why would he lie?"

"Probably just grief," said Jones, putting her handbag in a cupboard before locking it away. "The whole not speaking ill of the dead thing. You should have seen him after you died. He was beside himself. If he didn't truly love you, he is a very impressive actor."

Jones had pulled open the ledger they found last night, and started working her way backwards through it.

"Well, yes, perhaps you're right," said Autumn. She was prancing up and down in front of the counter, gesturing as she went. "But that is actually beside the point. My main point is that I seem to have a much deeper sense of the energy around me, and ever since Wren mentioned the fact that my death may be murder, I've had a stronger and stronger feeling that she is right."

"You have?" asked Jones, looking up from the ledger that she was trying to discern for possible clues.

"Yes, I have. I don't think my death was an accident, and I think we must see the police as soon as possible." Autumn stood in front of her sister, hands on her hips, like a school teacher disciplining a classroom.

"You're really sure. You're sure it wasn't an accident?" asked Jones. Autumn nodded rapidly in the affirmative.

"Alright, well, I'm sure we can fit it in today," said Jones. "Do you mean you'll come too? Is that wise after last night?"

"I'll be fine," said Autumn. "I think if I stick close to you, it will be ok. I was pondering it overnight, and like The Bank, I think you are one of my energy sources, perhaps just not quite as strong." Autumn put her hands out in front of her and began circling her arms, appearing to be conducting the energy in the room.

"Well, if you think so. But don't push it ok. If you need to head back to The Bank, just tell me and we'll leave straight away." Jones continued turning the pages of the ledger. She was determined to go through it with a fine tooth comb, on the lookout for any red flags in the days before Autumn's death.

"Of course, of course," said Autumn, who seemed to have relaxed a little now that Jones had agreed to go to the police station today. "Now, chop chop, doors will be opening very soon."

Jones looked at her watch and saw it was three minutes to nine already. She'd told Atlas to come in a little later today. He could have a sleep-in after all the work he'd put in.

The first few hours were slow. Jones had the opportunity to open a new lockbox for a customer. It was exciting for Jones, and with Autumn's help, she managed to get through the process with ease. The man was thrilled. He was excited that all his grandparents' letters were now kept somewhere safe. He was so worried his children would just throw them out one day. Jones wondered what would happen to them after he passed away, but due to the confidentiality of The Memory Bank, she didn't ask.

Jones also helped a young girl set herself up with everything she needed to start bullet journaling. It was one of the best things Jones had learnt years ago, at a workshop her father had held in The

Memory Bank when she was at University. Jones had used bullet journalling ever since to keep herself organised. It was particularly useful as a journalist. Plus, she had learnt, to a beginner level only, how to do some of the lovely drawings and calligraphy that some of the best bullet journalers used. It was fun to share this with her customer. Maybe she could host a bullet journal workshop in The Memory Bank one day. Perhaps another workshop on the note-taking skills she had learnt as a journalist. Jones was surprised to notice her mind pinging ideas in a flurry, planning future events for The Memory Bank. The future.

Atlas arrived just before eleven and headed straight to the computers. However, first, he thanked Jones for the whiskey from last night. "I felt like a bit of a celebrity when Hugo walked up and told me someone had bought me a drink!" Jones smiled, but she was pulled away by another enthusiastic customer.

As soon as The Memory Bank was empty for a moment, Jones went up to Atlas and made sure to thank him in person.

"Atlas, just in case I haven't made it clear, I cannot thank you enough for all your help in these last few weeks. There is just no way I could have reopened The Memory Bank without your help."

Atlas looked shocked, and a little embarrassment showed on his cheeks. He couldn't hold back a smile and nodded, whilst quietly saying "thank you, you are very welcome." Jones didn't want to make the moment more awkward, so she just smiled and walked away.

"I think that meant a lot to him," said Autumn, meeting Jones in the far corner of the room.

"Do you think? I hope so. I don't want him to think I don't appreciate everything he's done." Jones was taking a moment to stare out the window at The Memory Bank's rear garden, enjoying the current lull in customers requiring her assistance.

"He knows," said Autumn. "And don't forget, you've done a lot for him too. You've given him a great opportunity, and he's thoroughly enjoyed himself."

"He has, hasn't he," Jones said. She smiled at Autumn and, upon hearing the main door open again, made her way back to the retail area.

At lunchtime, Jones managed to find a minute to sit down with the ledger. She lugged it over to one of the tables near the rear windows, with Autumn hovering over her shoulder.

Most of the notes in the ledger were just everyday records. Lockboxes opened, books sold, and low stock needed to be replenished. But there was one note that caught their eye.

Schedule urgent stocktake of lockboxes.

"What was this about?" asked Jones

"I don't know," said Autumn. "From what I can recall, an urgent stocktake would have been quite unusual. It was a task I usually did in January. But look, the date is only a few weeks before my death. Do you think it may have had something to do with it?"

"At this point Autumn, I think we have to assume that anything out of the ordinary is a clue."

"So, what do we do?"

"I think you're right, I think we need to visit the police station. The sooner the better, because honestly, if your death was a murder, then the only thing I know for sure is that your killer is still out there."

The pair stared at each other in silence, absorbing the fact that it was appearing more and more likely that Autumn was murdered, and they had no idea why or by whom.

Jones asked Atlas if he was happy to man the shop by himself for a while. He beamed. "Sure thing boss!"

"No need to call me boss!" said Jones. "But as we've mentioned, you won't be able to do anything with the lockboxes while I'm out. I just need to be extra cautious about them at this stage. I'll train you up to do that eventually though if you want?"

"Yes," said Atlas. "That would be amazing."

"Perfect," said Jones. "Well if anyone comes in, let them know I should be back in an hour."

Atlas saluted Jones with a grin and moved off to grab another pile of documents that he was attempting to digitise.

With Autumn at her side, Jones strode out of The Memory Bank and towards the police station, on their quest to solve the mystery of her sister's death.

CHAPTER 9

Autumn followed Jones out the door and then went zooming ahead.

"Autumn, slow down!" Jones said as she got to the zebra crossing. Autumn was already halfway across, unaware that the speed she was capable of as a ghost was so much more than Jones could manage.

"Sorry," said Autumn, as Jones crossed the road. "Sorry, I didn't realise I could travel so fast. I'm just anxious to get to the police station and find out what's happening."

Jones was puffing and had to take a moment to catch her breath, leaning her arms against one of the London Plane Trees lining the street. "I know, I know. Are you sure you can get as far as the police station? How are you feeling?"

"I'm determined to," said Autumn, hands on her hips and lifting her chin. "Plus, I'm feeling amazing this morning. No idea why, but it's like I've had an extra big recharge."

"Ok, ok," said Jones. She took a long, deep breath to regroup. "But just a little slower from now on. You know, for the living amongst us!"

The police station was only a few hundred metres up the road. It looked just like a small red brick house, with a bullnose verandah out the front. Yet, it was signed with the bright blue police sign, opening hours and other notices pinned on and around the timber front door.

"What was his name?" Jones muttered under her breath, as they walked up the cement walkway to the door, desperately trying to remember the name of the local policeman. "Sergeant ah, Sergeant oh golly why can't I remember?"

"Sergeant Schmidt," said Autumn.

Jones snapped her eyes to Autumn. "How did you know that?" Autumn hadn't been around immediately after her death. Surely she didn't know who the policeman was who'd had almost daily contact with Jones during that time? Unless perhaps they'd met before her death, which Jones conceded was a possibility.

"It's here on the door! Sergeant Christopher Schmidt." Autumn laughed.

Jones rolled her eyes. "Ok, nice work detective. Now, just a reminder. Can you please not distract me when we get inside? I do *not* need to sound like a lunatic!"

"Sure, sure," Autumn grinned broadly and then signalled for Jones to lead the way. She opened the door.

A fan thunked round and round behind the counter. It was a sterile room. Grey laminate floors, grey laminate bench top, and a row of connected, grey plastic seats on one wall. Posters on gun safety, how to pay fines, and what numbers to call when you needed police but it wasn't an emergency, were all stuck to the walls with blue tac or sticky tape. Some posters had corners that were curling, and others were completely washed out, having been in front of the window for a long time.

No one was behind the counter. Jones walked up and looked for a device to signal her presence. A doorbell was stuck to the countertop, a small sticker next to it saying "Press for Help". Jones pressed, having absolutely no idea if it had worked or not.

Jones took a deep breath and then attempted to appear calm as she waited for someone to arrive. She was scanning her eyes across the many posters before gasping. Autumn was behind the counter! Jones was about to scold her sister when there was a large clunk, and a heavy door on the wall behind the counter was pushed open.

"Miss Eldershaw? How can I help you?" A tall, slim man walked into the room. His blonde hair was cut short, and despite the familiarity, his face remained calm but serious.

Jones was relieved to see that it was Sergeant Schmidt, the policeman who had spoken to her numerous times after Autumn's death. He'd always seemed nice, and Jones felt comfortable speaking with him. She relaxed a little.

"Hello Sergeant Schmidt," said Jones. She gave a slight smile before saying, "I just had a couple of questions about Autumn's case, if you don't mind?"

"Not at all," said Schmidt, nodding, and maintaining a serious look on his face. "I'll try and help if I can."

"I realised that I never asked," said Jones. "But is there any reason at all to consider that Autumn's death may have been anything other than an accident?"

Sergeant Schmidt didn't take his eyes off her, but he paused for quite a while. "Well, of course, all possibilities are considered when someone passes away," he said calmly.

"Yes," said Jones. "I do understand that. But in my sister's particular situation, was there any specific concern that there may have been more to her death than accidentally falling down the stairs?"

"Well now," said Sergeant Schmidt. "I can't exactly recall but perhaps I could look at her file?"

"Yes," said Jones. "Yes, that would be great."

Sergeant Schmidt paused, looking at Jones, and she wondered if she had missed a question.

"You'd like me to do that now?" he asked.

"Yes please," said Jones. "I presume that's possible?"

"Sure," he said, "not a problem at all. I'll take a quick look." Sergeant Schmidt walked back through the rear door, appearing happy to look into Jones's questions, although the tone of his voice made Jones feel as though her request was in fact a huge problem.

Jones let herself relax for a moment, turning to see the expression on her sister's face. She was surprised to discover Autumn wasn't there. Jones spun around, frantically trying to spot her sister. She caught a glimpse of Autumn's foot and the bottom of her red trench coach just as she passed through the wall into the rear of the station.

"Autumn," Jones thought. "What on earth are you doing?"

On the back of the wall was a small mirrored window, with narrow horizontal lines of clear glass. Jones leant on the front counter and tried her best to peer through the glass to see what was happening. It was useless. She occasionally saw movement but couldn't tell who it was or what they were doing. Jones shook her head and wondered if she was going to get any answers today.

Sergeant Schmidt seemed to take a rather long time to 'quickly' look at Autumn's file. Jones decided she would take that as a good sign and did her best to wait patiently. It would have been nice if she was able to also whisper *impatiently* to Autumn but she was anxious to discover what Autumn was doing back there.

Finally, the large door clicked open and Sergeant Schmidt was back. Autumn was not behind him.

"Unfortunately Miss Eldershaw, the case is still open so I'm unable to tell you anything further," said Sergeant. Schmidt.

"You can call me Jones," she replied. "I don't understand. If my sister's death was ruled an accident, why would it still be open?"

"Look, this is not my case anymore. It was referred to another branch and I don't have access to that information."

Jones shook her head, feeling very confused. "Moved to another branch? Why?"

"I'm sorry. I can't tell you that."

"Well, then who can? This is my sister's death after all. I have a right to know!" Jones felt her temper getting the better of her, and clutched her hands together to keep herself composed. "Would I be right in assuming that if the case is still open, then Autumn's death hasn't been completely ruled an accident?" Jones realised she may be pushing her luck, but thought it was worth a try.

"Look Miss Eldershaw," he replied, before speaking in a kinder tone. "Jones. I have to be very careful here, but I realise it's important you find out what is going on." Sergeant Schmidt moved forward, almost as though he was confiding in her. "All I can tell you is, your sister's case is related to another open case."

"It is?" Jones pulled her chin back and frowned. How could it be related to another case?

"Yes," said Sergeant Schmidt. "And because of this, I cannot tell you any more. As far as I am aware, your sister's case was determined an accident. If there is anything more to it, well that has not been disclosed in the information I have. The only thing I can do is look into it for you and see what I can find out."

"Well thank you," said Jones. "I think that would be the best thing to do. I'd appreciate it."

"You're welcome," said Sergeant Schmidt. "Is there anything else I can help you with?" His face had returned to a look of seriousness.

During their conversation, Autumn had reemerged from through the wall. Jones could see her trying to signal something, but did her best to ignore her. The last person she wanted to look strange and awkward in front of was the person she was relying on to get information on her sister's case.

"No, I think that's everything. Thanks for your, ah, help." Jones hadn't wanted to be rude, but at this stage Sergeant Schmidt had been no help whatsoever.

Jones turned to leave the station and saw Autumn waving frantically at her through the window. "What on earth does she know?" Jones wondered, rushing out the door.

CHAPTER 10

As Jones exited the station, she found her sister jogging on the spot, if ghosts could in fact jog. It was more of a floating run, the kind that Olympic sprinters seemed able to do.

"What in the world is the matter?" asked Jones.

"You aren't going to believe what I saw in my file!" Autumn said pushing her arms into the air.

"You read your file?" gasped Jones.

Autumn gestured for Jones to follow her back down the street.

"Of course I did! What did you think I was doing?" Autumn called over her shoulder as she flew down the street.

"I have absolutely no idea," said Jones. "Slow down! Slow down please."

Autumn rapidly pulled herself up. They were standing outside of Prue's office and, when realising her mistake, Autumn continued a few steps further until they could stand in a wall-lined driveway, apparently in the hope of making Jones talking to herself a little less conspicuous.

"So, you were looking at your own file?" prompted Jones.

"Yes! And do you know whose names I saw on there? Clancy! *And* Jamie!" Autumn stood there, hands on hips and eyes wide.

Jones turned her head, looking sideways at Autumn and said "Well that's not all that surprising. I mean Jamie was your boyfriend and Clancy used to work in The Bank."

"No, you don't understand. They weren't on a list of witnesses," said Autumn. "They were on a list of suspects!"

Jones's felt her face turn grey. She quickly put her hand on the plastered wall next to her, anticipating that her next move may be to slide down it.

"What? You have got to be kidding me!" said Jones. "So they did think you were killed! And you're saying Clancy *and* Jamie were on the suspects' list?"

"I am not kidding. I saw it as plain as day. Sergeant Schmidt left the file open on that page for quite a while. I think he was trying to work out what to say to you," said Autumn.

"What else was on the page?" asked Jones.

"A lot of gumph I didn't understand, but one thing written on that page was 'possible homicide?' with a question mark."

"Oh my god," Jones breathed. She felt her legs wobble but managed to keep standing.

"Yep," said Autumn. "It was a homicide investigation. At least at some point. Wren was right. I reckon she had more than a hunch. She just can't tell us. What if one of her clients told her something?"

Jones was resting her hands on her knees and taking deep breaths to compose herself.

"No!" said Jones, breathing deeply. "Surely not. I mean she only does wills and things, right? No, I think she just heard whispers around town." Jones slowly pushed herself up and leaned back against the wall.

"You're probably right," said Autumn. "I mean if the police were investigating a murder, there must be some good reason why. But what?"

"And who?" said Jones, taking one more long, deep breath.

"Exactly," said Autumn. "Come on, we'd better move." Autumn went to put her arm around Jones and promptly waved her arm straight through her sister's body. She balked for a moment before saying "Let's go. You're probably looking super weird right now."

"I feel super weird right now," said Jones. She felt lightheaded and wasn't even sure she could walk. She did it anyway. It was better to get back to The Memory Bank and time her collapse there.

"How cool is this ghost stuff though," said Autumn, twirling in front of Jones as she walked. "I mean I can literally walk through walls and look over shoulders!!"

Jones couldn't help but laugh. She was right. It was pretty cool. Perhaps this ghost stuff could be useful after all. All Jones knew was, she was going to get answers one way or another. And Autumn would be the perfect person to assist.

CHAPTER 11

Realising she should eat lunch on her lunch break, Jones quickly went into The Lilly Pilly Pantry and picked up a chicken caesar salad roll. They then walked briskly (well, Autumn floated and twirled) back to The Memory Bank to relieve Atlas.

"How did you go?" Jones asked as she walked up to the counter. There were a few customers dotted around the shop, and Atlas had just finished ringing up another customer. Jones felt her hands shaking just a little. The pressure of trying not to completely flip was getting to her, but she kept her composure. Food and a seat would no doubt help.

"No problems," said Atlas. "There was one person who came in wanting to put something into their lockbox but they were happy to come back later this afternoon. I think they were going to come at about three. Otherwise, we've had a few sales and everyone seems happy."

"Thank you Atlas," said Jones. "Great work!" She hoped she appeared supportive and enthusiastic, and not as though she wanted to rush through this conversation so she could go and talk to Autumn.

Autumn was gliding in and out of the bookshelves on the far side of the room. Jones could tell she was waiting to speak to her and attempted to casually walk through the store, stopping to chat with a few of the customers, and answering one question about a pack of Washi tape and how people used it in journalling.

Eventually, she got to one of the tables near the rear garden where Autumn was standing. Jones took a seat and began to unwrap her caesar salad roll.

"Jones!" Autumn said, much louder than expected.

"Shhh!" Jones hissed.

"No one can hear me!"

"I know," said Jones, rolling her eyes. "But I need to whisper, so I need you to whisper too."

"Oh-kay," Autumn said, rolling her eyes back at Jones, but turning her volume down. "So, what are we going to do?"

"I just can't believe Clancy and Jamie are suspects! Why would either of them want to murder you?" Jones took a large bite of her roll and chewed, wiping some of the sauce off her chin.

"They were suspects," said Autumn. "Maybe my death was an accident. Maybe nothing came of the investigation. But if I was murdered, then I have no idea why they would be considered suspects," said Autumn, floating a figure eight in front of Jones's table.

"I mean, I suppose it isn't all that surprising that Jamie, as your boyfriend, would be considered a suspect. Isn't that automatic?" said Jones.

"I suppose so," said Autumn, shrugging but not looking completely convinced. "So what about Clancy? I mean it seems so unlikely, but Jamie mentioned Clancy too. Does he know something?"

"It must be something to do with Clancy's connection to The Memory Bank," said Jones, taking another bite, chewing with her eyes closed. Once she had finished her mouthful, her eyes flicked open. "So perhaps the answer is right here!" Jones put her hands flat on the table and stood up quickly, pushing her chair away from the table.

"Right here?" asked Autumn. "What do you mean?"

"The ledgers of course!" said Jones, a little too loudly. She froze and looked at Autumn, panicking that someone might have heard her.

"It's ok," said Autumn, looking over Jones's shoulder. "I don't think anyone noticed."

"Phew," said Jones. "So, the ledgers. Things about Clancy would be in the ledgers from Dad's time too. Not only the ones just before your death. Maybe the note in the ledger we saw *was* about a meeting you had scheduled with Clancy. But why? There was no other reference to him there. So it has to be something to do with before he left The Bank don't you think? Maybe we've been looking in the wrong place!"

"Oh my gosh," said Autumn. "You're right!'

"Do we know exactly where they are, the old ledgers?" asked Jones.

"I have no idea. I've never needed to look at them," said Autumn. "They could be in any of the filing cabinets in the basement."

"I bet Atlas knows," said Jones.

Jones strode over to the counter, Autumn following closely behind. Atlas was busy typing into the computer, living his commitment to digitising all the records of The Memory Bank.

"Atlas," said Jones. "I've just been thinking about a few things and thought I might take a look at some of the ledgers from when Dad was here. I don't suppose you've digitised those yet?"

"No I haven't," said Atlas. "I'm still working through Autumn's records, but I'm getting close to finishing those. Did you need me to make a start on them?" Atlas lifted his glasses and rubbed his eye.

"No, you're doing an amazing job. You've already entered so much!" said Jones. "But perhaps you can point me in the direction of Dad's ledgers. I'm quite happy to look through the originals."

Atlas pushed himself away from the counter, his chair rolling backwards. "I'll go and grab them for you if you like. I need a break! How far back do you want me to go?"

"Ah, well, I'm not sure?" Jones was needing Autumn's help on this one but didn't want to turn and look at her. Thankfully Autumn got the message and whispered "I think the last five years will be enough. It wasn't long before I started that Clancy finished."

"Perhaps, the last five years before Autumns started," said Jones. "If that's not too much?"

"Sure thing!" Atlas jumped off his chair and walked away towards the basement.

For some reason, Jones felt herself becoming anxious. She couldn't quite put her finger on why. It was as though she knew she was going to find something disturbing inside the ledgers. They were the ledgers that recorded all the mundane information about The Memory Bank, the bland day-to-day business information of The Bank. So why did it feel like she had something stuck in her throat? Why now and not yesterday when Wren told her Autumn had been murdered? Why not before her trip to the police station? Why was the thought of going through her father's ledgers the thing that was making her feel nervous and a little panicky? It wasn't as though she expected to see "Autumn was murdered by…." written in bold red ink on one of the pages.

Atlas returned, holding five large and heavy leather-covered ledges. "Where shall I put them?" Jones could see he was very ready to put them down!

"Oh ah," said Jones. "Put them on the other side of the counter. I'll sit around there and keep out of your way." That way Jones could hopefully still whisper to Autumn as they went through them, but be available to help with customers as needed.

As Jones pulled out the most recent ledger, Autumn came and sat on the counter, almost on top of the ledger.

"Give me some space," whispered Jones.

"Oh come on, you can just put your arm right through me!"

Jones shuddered. She realised that although she knew Autumn was a ghost, she still thought of her sister as a living and breathing person. The idea of putting her arm right through her sister horrified her. Autumn seemed to register the horror on Jones's face and scooched herself away slightly.

Jones flicked through the ledger, looking for Clancy's name, or anything else that seemed to hint at the possible connection between Clancy and Autumn's death. The first ledger contained absolutely nothing, not a single mention of Clancy.

"It looks like he'd already left The Bank," said Autumn. Jones nodded and opened the next ledger.

As Jones turned these pages, going from front to back, Clancy's name started to pop up. Just a few references to jobs he'd done around The Memory Bank. It seems he was in charge of all the maintenance and the day-to-day operations of The Bank. He also appeared to have responsibility for the lockboxes, with her father recording how many were opened or created by himself or Clancy, and who had been responsible for managing the access to the lockboxes. It seemed Clancy did most of this.

"He had quite a bit of responsibility," said Autumn, sounding somewhat surprised.

Jones thought so too, but then remembered that she had also promised Atlas he could start working with the lockboxes eventually. She trusted Atlas to do the right thing, so her father must have trusted Clancy too.

Jones kept flicking through but was also a little distracted as she tried to work out why someone who her father trusted so much could have ended up on a list of suspects in Autumn's murder. It was surely a mistake. Maybe it wasn't that he was a suspect. Maybe it was just that Autumn's death did have something to do with The Memory Bank, and the police had been speaking to him to get information on how it worked. Of course, at that stage, he was the only one left who knew anything about The Memory Bank.

"Maybe we should ask Clancy to come and visit The Bank?" whispered Jones "You know, give him a tour, and then just ask him a few general questions. The police thought your death may have been connected to The Bank. Perhaps he had some information."

Jones turned to look at her sister, to see what she thought of the idea.

Autumn raised her eyebrows. "I doubt he'd show his face here."

"What do you mean?"

"Well, because Dad fired him."

"What?" Jones was shocked, and then she saw her sister pointing at an entry on the page Jones had just turned to.

There it was, written literally in black and white.

Clancy Tupper fired. Police involved.

"Oh my gosh!" said Jones.

Jones quickly flicked the ledger to see what else might have been written in there. There was not another single entry referencing Clancy after this date.

"Autumn, do you know anything about this?" Jones hissed, still reeling from this ledger entry.

"No!" she said. "I don't think Dad ever told me. At least not that I can remember. It was well before I started working here full-time. But now I think about it, hmm...." Autumn slowly floated off the counter and started staring into the distance.

"What? What?" Jones whispered, frantically, following her sister over to the very end of The Memory Bank where it was empty and quiet.

"It's just, now that I think of it, every time Clancy's name came up in conversation, Dad's face turned to thunder. I remember knowing not to ask him anything because he wouldn't say a thing. I just stopped mentioning Clancy. After a while, it didn't matter. I started taking over more and more. Dad never spoke of Clancy again, so I have no idea what it was about."

"I'm going to have to speak to him," said Jones, putting her hands on her hips.

"No, you can't! It says police were involved. What if it's too dangerous?" Autumn's eyes were wide. She certainly looked scared.

"Well what do you suggest I do?" asked Jones. "I've already been to the police. They won't tell me anything!"

"Jones it might not have anything to do with my death. I mean I was still in high school when this happened. I only worked part-time on the weekends or after school, and I don't recall Clancy being around much. I can't see how it would have anything to do with my death."

Jones shook her head. "Autumn, I don't know what I'm going to find, but this is the only lead we have. I have to follow it."

"Only lead," Autumn almost laughed. "What, are you a detective now?"

Jones laughed a little too, but then seriously "Well, it seems you and I are the only people doing anything, so yes, I'm now a detective!"

"Well, then I am too!" said Autumn. "The Eldershaw Sisters Detective Agency!"

Jones smiled at Autumn. The image of herself as a detective was funny. Picturing herself in a hat, holding a briefcase, solving "The Case of the Death of Autumn Eldershaw". As Jones thought about it further, she realised it wasn't such a stretch, her being a detective, especially after having a career as a journalist. Being a journalist was often exactly like being a detective, trying to source quotes, new insights, and information no one else had been able to find. She couldn't claim to be like the investigative journalists of true crime podcasts who did solve mysteries, but the skills were there.

"Right," said Jones. "I'm going to call Clancy and arrange to meet him. Then I need to go and help Atlas. I've done nothing all day!"

It didn't take long for Jones to find Clancy's phone number online. He answered immediately and was quite happy for Jones to come and visit him that evening. Especially as she told him that she was hoping to pick his brain about running The Memory Bank. It was a fact that if Autumn hadn't been around, she would have reached out to Clancy anyway, so she hoped the request didn't make him in any way suspicious.

"Jones," Autumn continued to follow Jones around The Bank. "Do you think you should bring Wren? Or someone? For safety?"

Jones attempted to tidy the family history bookshelves without appearing like a crazy person talking to herself.

"I'll be fine! Clancy is harmless," said Jones.

"Really?" said Autumn. "He was on a list of suspects for my murder. Let's perhaps assume he is at least slightly less than harmless." Autumn had started hovering on the other side of the shelf, disconcertingly popping her head through the books Jones was organising.

"Ok," said Jones. "I get your point. But I don't think we should bring anyone else into it at this stage. If it is dangerous, and perhaps you're right, I don't want Wren involved."

Autumn rolled her eyes at Jones.

"So, it will just be the two of us?" said Autumn. "One of us being a ghost. Great idea Jones." Autumn projected her sarcasm through the bookshelf beautifully. Her head and accompanying eye roll followed her.

"Don't worry about me. But *you're* coming?" said Jones. "Can you make it that far? Don't you think it would be better to conserve your energy and stay at The Bank? I mean there's not much you'll be able to do."

Autumn couldn't hide the hurt on her face. "Do you really think you're going to leave one-half of The Eldershaw Sisters Detective Agency out of the picture? I think not! I may not be able to 'do' much, but I can snoop like no one else. Don't forget the power of having a ghost on your side. How many other detectives have a partner who can walk through walls, and peer over shoulders without being noticed!"

"Ok, ok," Jones whispered, moving on to neatening up the shelves of paper. "You can come. Now can you leave me alone? I've seen Atlas glance at me a few times. He either thinks I'm weird or not pulling my weight. So let me do my job!"

Autumn grinned and then glided off to peer over Atlas's shoulder and see what he was entering from her ledgers.

Jones stared after her sister. She was surprised that her sister appeared to be taking seriously the idea of the Eldershaw Sisters Detective Agency. Jones smiled and then felt a sudden throb of pain in her heart. The idea of teaming up was so appealing to Jones, but of course, it was a ridiculous thought. Her sister was a ghost. She was dead. And there was no way of knowing exactly how long they would remain together.

Jones and Autumn had never really been a team. They had always been different, almost opposites. Any teamwork as sisters was forced upon them as they had to get through school and all the extracurricular activities that went with it, whilst their father worked to look after their small family.

The older they got the more distance there was between them. Autumn spent more and more time helping her father, front of house at The Memory Bank. Jones was absorbed in her schoolwork and got the best possible grades she could. Autumn was also very social, part of many clubs and organisations. Jones continued to play netball throughout high school, but other than that, she had a few close friends she would spend time with, just hanging out at each other's houses.

The idea that Autumn's death, possibly murder, was the thing that brought them back together made her heart ache. Not even their father's death had had this effect. They were too busy getting 'back to normal', and making the most of their careers at that time. Why did it seem that the best part of their relationship was just starting, and yet, Autumn was dead?

CHAPTER 12

The lock clanked shut, and Jones and Autumn walked out into the warm, late afternoon. With daylight saving, it was still very light at six o'clock. A few cars were driving past, and Jones saw a couple walk into Hugo's. Jones did glance that way and briefly wonder if she had time for a quick drink, but decided against it. She didn't want alcohol muddling her brain even slightly. Jones knew she needed to be switched on for this meeting with Clancy.

Jones was holding a notebook and a pen that she had selected from The Memory Bank stock. She had chosen a gorgeous turquoise Rhodia soft-cover notebook with its signature orange elastic, along with a white Kaweco rollerball pen. She had never had such expensive stationery when she had worked as a journalist and wondered why. Why had she always bought cheap Bic pens and Spirax notebooks when she had access to all this amazing product? Was she living the life of what she thought a journalist was supposed to be? I mean, she never saw any of her colleagues toting around fancy stationery. Yet, Jones had always prided herself on being a little unique, a little unusual. Her style of tailored pants, grandma cardigans, and quirky t-shirts was part of that. Combined with white sneakers and her crossbody handbag, she felt comfortable in her own skin and confident to venture out into the world of journalism.

Autumn on the other hand was a lot more vibrant in her style. She always leant towards flowy dresses, camisoles and blazers, heels or boots, and loved styling her red hair. Autumn's personality was also a lot more vibrant than her sister's. Jones was one to have a quiet one-on-one conversation at a party, whilst Autumn was usually in the middle of a large, noisy, laughing group.

Tonight was a little different. Autumn was keeping close and quiet. She had tried to explain to Jones how energy seemed to work as a ghost. Autumn had a theory that the only way she existed was due to the energy of things important to her. The Memory Bank and her sister seemed to be the most powerful. In fact, it seemed The Memory Bank was the source of her energy but she could tap into Jones's energy when she needed to, although it wasn't as powerful, and seemed to have a time limit. Autumn had decided tonight to do her best to conserve her energy, or, to be more accurate, Jones's energy so that she could reach Clancy's and stay with Jones for as long as possible. However, they had agreed that if Autumn started to feel weak she would make it very clear that she needed to head back to The Memory Bank as quickly as possible. Neither of them had any idea what would happen if Autumn lost too much energy. They couldn't bear to consider it.

Clancy lived on the very edge of town, on the opposite side to The Memory Bank. It had once been quite a grand home, but as Jones and Autumn walked up to the front, they could see that things had been let go. Ivy was covering the front of the house, and much of the door. The hedges were overgrown, and the lawn was brown and patchy. Roses that once lined the front fence were unruly, covered in dead blooms. Weeds grew through the paving stones leading up to the house, and the slate steps were broken and out of place.

Jones wasn't quite sure whether to use the large brass door knocker but opted to tap cautiously on the leadlight glass, which was still in surprisingly good condition on either side of the timber door. Autumn wanted to just slide on through the door, but Jones stopped her. She at least wanted to do things properly to start with. Autumn could wander through the house at her leisure once they were invited inside. Well, once Jones was invited in.

Just as Jones was about to try the knocker, she heard shuffling footsteps coming towards the door. It was opened, and there stood Clancy. His white hair had been slicked down, and he had obviously tried to make himself presentable. He wore a striped shirt and navy slacks, both of which had seen better days, food stains and patched knees showing. On his feet were the same grandpa shoes she had seen him wearing. Jones did her best not to stare and smiled at Clancy.

"Jones! It was a lovely surprise to hear from you. Come in, come in," and Clancy stepped to the side, arm extended, inviting Jones in. The hallway was quite empty. There was a hall stand and Jones could see at one point the walls had been covered in photos or paintings, but they had been removed. White squares of clean paint were all that remained. The first thing that hit her was the smell. It wasn't awful, but it was musty, almost mouldy, with some unidentifiable fragrance that seemed to permeate the homes of the elderly. As they walked Jones tried to peer into the rooms on either side, but most of the doors were shut or the rooms were dark. Why she thought this was important she didn't know, once she realised that Autumn had already left her side and was flitting in and out of each room ahead of them.

The house was large, but Clancy brought them through the kitchen and into a very small sunroom at the back. A fan on a stand was ticking its way through its rotation, causing a few papers on a sideboard to flutter under a paperweight. Clancy had his recliner which was set up with small side tables on either side holding books and mugs and plates. Pushed to the side was a table on which he had clearly been eating his dinner.

Clancy pointed at a kitchen chair, indicating for Jones to take a seat.

"Now, can I get you anything? A cup of tea perhaps?" he asked.

To be polite, and because in that instant she did feel like a cup of tea, Jones agreed. She felt nervous about how clean the teacup may be but decided to risk life and limb at this early stage in the 'interview'.

"That would be lovely," she said. "White with one, please."

Whilst Clancy shuffled off to the kitchen, Jones took the time to look around the room from her seat. A collection of odd furniture had been shoved into the room, struggling to fit. There was a wooden filing cabinet, piled high with papers that she presumed couldn't fit inside. A rolltop desk exploding with books and knick-knacks. Even more items were lodged in bookshelves, next to an old telephone stand with the classic brown vinyl-covered seat. An old television was propped on top of a set of drawers, framed by a large number of dusty photographs. Various boxes and baskets on the floor were filled with papers and notebooks. Plus, random chairs dotted the room, all with items piled on them or hanging from the back. It didn't leave much space in the room, and Jones recognised this was the place Clancy spent most of his time.

Autumn made her way into the room. "Are you ok?" she whispered. "I'm just scouting the location if you're ok on your own?" Jones wasn't quite sure if her sister's detective lingo was on point, but she smiled and nodded in approval. Who knew what Autumn might find? It was unlikely there was going to be a room filled with evidence about her death. Yet, Jones had to admit it certainly couldn't hurt to use the unique skills of a ghost to gather as much information as possible.

Clancy came back with a mismatched set of mugs and a teapot, along with a jug of milk and a sugar bowl. It was all very old-fashioned but Jones liked it and, thankfully, everything seemed perfectly clean. Jones went ahead and poured her cup before settling back into her chair. Sitting there holding a cup of tea in a flowery mug was quite incongruous with the idea of Clancy having killed her sister.

"Now," said Clancy. "You wanted to chat about The Memory Bank?" After pouring the tea he had sat with a 'flump' back into his recliner.

"Yes," said Jones. "I'd love to hear about your time at The Bank. When did you start working with my father?" She sipped her tea, doing her best to appear calm and casual.

"Well, now let me think. I believe I worked for him for nearly ten years, so can you work that one out?"

Ten years, thought Jones. She hadn't expected it to be quite that long. What went so wrong that her father had to fire him?

"What year did you leave?" she asked, despite knowing exactly when he left, or more accurately when he was *asked to leave*.

"Golly, now you're testing an old man," said Clancy. "Your father was a wonderful man. Lovely to work for. We achieved a lot together actually. The Memory Bank had gotten quite run down. It was hard on your Dad you know after your Mum died. He had a lot on his plate. Worked very hard and looked after you girls. But he did all of it on his own for a long time so it was hard for him to keep on top of things. By the time he got me on to help, things had gotten away from him."

Jones smiled, genuinely interested, but not missing the fact that Clancy had deliberately changed the subject when she had asked what year he had left.

"So, what did you do at The Bank? What was your job?" Jones ran her hand over her notebook and wondered if she should at least pretend to take notes. She thought it best to play her role. Putting down her teacup, Jones opened her notebook and held her pen poised, ready.

"Well, I guess you'd call me a bit of a jack-of-all-trades. I'd fix things, did a lot of painting, renovated a lot of the time, you know stripping it back and sanding. The front door used to have layers and layers of paint on it before I got stuck into it."

"And did you help with customers too? Did you help with the lockboxes?" Jones desperately hoped she didn't sound too enthusiastic with her questioning. She wasn't supposed to be in journalist mode but realised she couldn't help herself.

"Oh yes, after a few years, once your father and I got settled together. He trained me in the process and I'd help people access their lockboxes or open new ones. What a great idea that was," smiled Clancy.

"What do you mean, the lockboxes?" asked Jones.

"Oh yes, they were a hit. I mean, of course, it was your grandmother who started those," said Clancy. "Everyone loved them. So many people stored their memories. But it wasn't just that. It encouraged people to start collecting their memories and sharing them. So much of the town's story, the history would have been lost if it wasn't for The Memory Bank. Have you had a look at all the memoirs on the shelf? Have you read them?"

Jones was a little embarrassed to admit she hadn't. She was also feeling a little embarrassed to have suspected Clancy of Autumn's murder. He seemed so enthusiastic about The Bank and all that it stood for.

"Well young lady, now that you are at the helm you really should," Clancy turned slightly in his recliner, trying to face her directly.

Jones couldn't help but smile at the enthusiasm and pride in Clancy's words. He was right, she needed to learn more about the history of The Memory Bank and Lilly Pilly Creek.

"I hear you've got an amazing shop in there now," Clancy continued. "That you're doing amazing things. Just don't forget what it was all about. The memories. The recording of memories. The sharing of memories." Clancy paused and turned to stare out the window. He was now clearly lost in his memories.

Jones sat still for a minute, taking in Clancy's words. They had struck her. She realised that perhaps in her hurry to get The Memory

---

Bank up to scratch for the opening, she had missed its bigger mission. Memories. She had to admit that she appreciated the words Clancy shared with her. That's why she hesitated with her next question. Yet, it was why she was here. She had to ask. Jones forced her journalist hat back on and leaned in just a little.

"Clancy, why did you stop working for my father?"

Clancy didn't move, didn't flinch, didn't turn away from the window. Jones wasn't sure he had heard her. Then eventually he turned, picked up his cup of tea, and took a long sip.

"Talking of memories," said Clancy.

"Oh?" asked Jones. She felt herself frown and quickly attempted to bring her expression back to neutral.

Clancy didn't look at her, but directly into his teacup. He began to speak.

"It's a memory I am ashamed of. It's a memory I wish I could forget. I wish I could lie to you Jones," he said, quickly glancing at Jones and then back to his cup. Jones saw Autumn glide back into the room. She had been listening from elsewhere in the house and realised this was the important part of the conversation.

"I have lied for many years, or just not spoken about it. Some people know, of course, many who haven't forgiven me, but they have pretended to forget."

"Forget what?" Jones was starting to feel that lump in her throat again. She wondered if she had done the right thing coming here. Should she leave or was it too late? But she just had to know the answer, no matter what. For Autumn's sake.

"I was desperately hoping I wouldn't have to have this conversation with you Jones. I'm deeply ashamed. I betrayed your father," said Clancy. "He trusted me and I took advantage of that."

Jones didn't say anything. She kept quiet, letting him speak. It was a journalism trick. Just let them feel they had to keep talking, to fill in the silence. It crossed her mind that she had seen this move in detective shows on television as well. If it had been a more appropriate situation, she would have laughed and told Autumn that perhaps she was turning into a detective after all. Instead, she waited for Clancy to continue.

"I used people's memories against them," said Clancy.

"What? How?" Now Jones was very confused. How could you use someone's memories against them?

"It started innocently enough," said Clancy, turning to once again stare out the window. "One day when I went to return a lockbox to its position, I saw that the client had left it unlocked. The Bank was empty. Everyone had gone home, including your father for once. Usually, he was the last to leave, but I had finally been able to encourage him to get home at a reasonable time, cook dinner for you and your sister, and get to bed early."

Jones had a sudden memory of sitting at the kitchen table with an older lady, not her father. She was dishing out quiche and salad which neither of the girls had liked. Jones had completely forgotten about Mrs Ackerman. Mrs Ackerman was a lady who would come and look after them when their father was at work. She'd make the sisters do their homework and cook dinner for them. Jones remembered her being a bit of a grump. Yet, there were times when it was her father, cooking them sausages and mashed potatoes, or fried eggs and chips.

"Jones" hissed Autumn. Jones snapped back to the present. What had Clancy just said?

"Instead of just locking the box and putting it away, I opened it," Clancy continued. "I shouldn't have. I wish I had never opened it. I was doing something completely against all policies. I was undermining the integrity of The Bank. But it was just a quick look. Who was going to know? I just started reading a letter that was on the top."

"Oh!" Jones exclaimed. She may not have as extensive knowledge of The Memory Bank as Autumn did, but she did know this. Never, ever, under any circumstances look in a client's lockbox. Even if they insisted, you were meant to decline. It was just too dangerous a line to cross when it came to trust and confidentiality.

Clancy continued his story, rubbing his thumbs over the back of his hands. "It was a letter that someone had written but never sent. And it revealed that the owner of the lockbox was having an affair. They were having an affair and the letter was confessing to their wife, but they had put it in their lockbox. "Clancy dared raise his head and look Jones in the eye. "The thing was, the lockbox belonged to someone well-known in the community and someone quite rich." Clancy paused.

"What did you do?" asked Jones.

"Well, I quickly put the lockbox away, shocked at what I had read. But I couldn't stop thinking about it." Clancy shook his head and sighed.

Jones took a sip of her tea and glanced at Autumn, on the edge of her seat. She felt like she was living inside a British murder mystery television show. How did this lead to her father firing Clancy? He surely didn't fire him for reading one letter.

"It was a bad time in my life. I wasn't in a good place. I was so frustrated and angry because my wife had left me a few years before that. Left me for another man. I was struggling. I was struggling emotionally, but I was also struggling financially because I was trying to buy her half of the house. The house we sit in now. She was demanding we sell the house but I refused. I loved this house. I had worked so hard for it. So I was trying to buy her out instead of selling. But it was pushing me to my limit."

Jones realised she was beginning to feel quite sorry for him. She thought about possibly having to sell her own family home, and the idea filled her with sadness. Unfortunately, it was looking like a decision she would have to make, one way or the other, and soon.

"And then someone, someone so important with such a reputation in the community, was having an affair and hurting another person. They were doing the wrong thing and weren't man enough, to tell the truth. So I confronted them. I told them that they had left the box open. Obviously, they wanted someone to find it. I told him I would tell his wife or he could pay me to keep his secret."

Jones gasped. "You blackmailed him?"

Clancy nodded his head and looked down at his hands which were trembling. She could see tears starting to brim in his eyes.

"Of course, he didn't want his wife to know," Clancy said after a significant pause. "And not surprisingly, he didn't have the guts to confess. He could only write a letter and lock it in a box. So he agreed to pay me. He didn't want it to be noticeable, so he would pay me a few hundred dollars every week. This happened for years. On occasion, he would beg me to stop, but I was cruel. I continued to blackmail him. I honestly still don't know what came over me. But it was such a relief to get that money. To pay my wife, knowing I could keep my house."

Jones simply didn't know what to think. She looked at Autumn who, raising her palms to the ceiling, indicated that she was just as shocked and confused as Jones.

"But of course, that wasn't enough, and I started looking into other people's lockboxes, unlocking them and reading their memories. The money I was getting wasn't enough to pay off the house, and it was so easy. Too easy. I didn't always find something I could use to blackmail someone, but when I did, I made the most of it. It became an addiction. By the time your father found out, I think I was blackmailing four different people."

"Really? Four!" Jones couldn't believe what she was hearing.

"Yes," said Clancy. His face was pale now, almost grey. Jones began to become concerned he might pass out. "Some people refused of course. I was just the impetus they needed to come clean about whatever it was. But most people were cowards and were happy to pay rather than have their secret come out. Eventually, I was easily able to pay back my wife, and I had enough cash to start doing some of the things I wanted to do. Travel, buy the car I had always wanted, it was amazing. But always, always, tinged with guilt, of betraying your father and becoming someone I just didn't recognise."

"You said that my Dad found out?" asked Jones, leaning further forward in her seat, pressing her hands into her knees.

"Yes," said Clancy. "The last person I tried to blackmail wasn't having any of it. He'd heard some rumours in the past, and then when I approached him, he realised it was true, and so he took advantage of the situation. He pretended to agree and asked me to put something in writing. I was getting arrogant. Nothing had ever gone wrong. So I did. This person went and spoke to another person I was blackmailing, someone who had previously said something about me. This second person confided in him, and so he had the information he needed to approach your father."

"What did Dad do?" Jones could only imagine how shocked he would have been. He wasn't one to lose his temper, but this was a very unusual situation.

"Well, he was furious, understandably," said Clancy. "He tore strips off me and fired me immediately."

"Did he go to the police?" Jones knew of course he did, it was written in the ledger after all.

"Oh, he was going to. Scared me to pieces. But I begged. I begged, and I'm sorry to admit it, I cried. Your father made me promise to pay everyone back. Every cent. If he heard that I had failed to do so within a reasonable time, he would go to the police." Clancy was clutching his hands together now, as though he was physically trying to hold himself together.

Jones nodded. Her father was a reasonable person, especially someone he had considered a friend. But she was surprised he didn't go to the police. This was very serious. How could he feel comfortable not bringing Clancy to justice? To put The Memory Bank at risk? Jones began to feel as though she didn't recognise her father.

"Well, as you may have noticed, this house is not in great shape." He looked up and waved his arm around the room. "I sold everything, well, almost everything, to pay them back. I didn't manage to pay everything back. Some of them died or told me we were square. But I did my best to make amends. I even continued to do so after your father died. People still despise me in this town, but I kept my promise to your father."

Clancy looked so sad. She was surprised. She was shocked. Yet, she couldn't quite see what this might have to do with Autumn's murder. Jones wasn't about to ask. She would need time to talk with Autumn, to work out what to do next.

"Did you often speak with my father after this?" Jones asked, wondering if something more recent might provide a clue.

"No," said Clancy. "Never. I was too ashamed." He stared down at his hands, closes his eyes and sighed.

"Jones," Autumn whispered. She had come back in. "Jones, ask him if he ever spoke to me."

Jones glanced up at her sister and raised her eyebrows. Autumn nodded and pointed towards Clancy. "Ask him."

"Did you ever speak with Autumn? With my sister?"

Clancy's eyes shot open and he took a deep breath. Then he shook his head. "No, I never did," he said, and once again closed his eyes. "I wish I had. I loved my work at The Bank. I've never felt content since."

Jones nodded and they both fell silent.

"Well, thank you for your time," said Jones, leaning back in her seat.

"Of course my dear," said Clancy. "I'm just so sorry I never made peace with your father before he died. It is one of the regrets of my life."

Jones nodded and stood up. "Don't get up," she said, waving her hand at Clancy. "I can show myself out."

When Jones had closed the door behind her and made it back to the footpath, Autumn was waiting. "Well, what did you think?"

"I'm a little shocked, to be honest," said Jones

"About the blackmail?" asked Autumn.

"Absolutely," said Jones. "Plus, I can't believe Dad didn't go to the police."

"Yes, but if he had, the whole business could have gone under. Imagine the community outcry!"

"But it wasn't Dad who did it," said Jones, rather loudly.

"No of course not," said Autumn. "But the trust would be obliterated. And you know that The Memory Bank only exists because people trust us. People would have removed their lockboxes, and no one would have ever returned."

Jones nodded and continued walking. "What I don't see is how it's connected to your murder. If at all," she said. "I just can't understand why Clancy was listed as a suspect?"

"I have no idea," said Autumn. "Perhaps I found out about the blackmail and threatened to expose him. I mean, it kind of sounds like something I'd do."

Jones smiled. It certainly sounded like her sister. Gung ho when it came to standing up for her principles.

"I don't think he's telling us everything," continued Autumn. 'I have a strong feeling he was hiding something. I just don't know what."

"He did tell us all about the blackmail. I barely even prompted him. It was like he was just waiting to tell us," said Jones. "He seems like a very sad, lonely, old man who has many regrets in his life."

Autumn and Jones continued walking in silence. It was dark, with no moonlight to shine the way. The occasional dog barked, and they saw a few evening walkers in the distance. Autumn said goodbye as they came to The Memory Bank, floating away through the wall, and Jones continued on home.

Jones couldn't help thinking more about what Autumn had said. What if Autumn had discovered the blackmail? Had she planned to take it to the police, and let Clancy know first? And after all this time, and all his work to pay back the money, was it something he was willing to kill for? Clancy seemed such a frail old man. It seemed impossible that he could have killed Autumn. Yet how much strength would it take to push someone down the stairs, especially if you got them off balance? Jones knew she couldn't exclude Clancy. She hated to admit it, but he was easily their strongest suspect.

However, she couldn't forget that there wasn't one, but two names under the list of suspects in Autumn's police file. Jamie. What on earth could he have to do with Autumn's death?

CHAPTER 13

As had become her routine, the next morning Jones pulled on one of her quirky t-shirts (today's read "She knew she could but she needed coffee first" which she was sure Sybil would appreciate) and then walked to pick up her morning cup.

Sybil most certainly appreciated Jones's t-shirt. "I think I might need to start a t-shirt collection like yours!"

"You could create Sybil's Coffee Van merchandise," said Jones. "I could create The Memory Bank merchandise!" The pair laughed, but Jones tucked the idea away.

As usual, Sybil had her unique style on display. Today her stone grey hair was twisted into two buns on either side of her head, and she wore a brightly knitted Jenny Kee jumper with a galah across the front. She looked glorious!

Jones chatted with Sybil for a few moments, as the hiss of the coffee machine steamed the full cream milk Sybil purchased direct from a local dairy farmer.

"Now Jones, I hope you're not too upset?" asked Sybil. Jones suddenly wondered if Sybil had heard about her meeting with Clancy and started to panic. How could she know?

"Upset? About what?"

"That nasty piece of work Prue Timberley."

"Oh her," Jones hoped she didn't sound too relieved. "You heard about her visit to The Bank I suppose. I'm not worried about that." Jones reached up and grasped the floral takeaway cup from Sybil's outstretched hand.

"So you haven't seen?" said Sybil, reaching to pat Frank the cat who had today taken up position in a basket of serviettes.

"Seen what exactly?" Jones was suddenly very concerned. What was Prue capable of? For some reason, Jones immediately pictured a for sale sign out the front of The Memory Bank. Jones knew it was ridiculous, but what else could it be?

"You'll see soon enough," said Sybil, who then turned to the next customer waiting in line. "But don't worry Jones, the whole town is behind you," Sybil called loudly, returning to steaming milk. "Well, almost the whole town." The last part was mumbled by Sybil, but Jones heard every word.

Jones stared at Sybil for a moment, trying desperately to decipher what she had told her. She couldn't fathom what Prue could have done, so she started walking briskly towards The Memory Bank, struggling to sip and not spill the hot coffee in her hurry.

Soon enough, as she came up to The Lilly Pilly Pantry, she saw them. Plastered all over the community notice board, covering every other piece of paper that had been pinned, were bright, glossy posters, depicting The Memory Bank, *her* Memory Bank, as a bustling community market. Jones froze, mouth wide open, coffee cup halfway up to her mouth.

The nerve! The absolute nerve! How dare she. Jones couldn't control herself and immediately ripped down the two posters in front of her. She left one lying shredded on the footpath, but the second one she scrunched up in her fist. She *had* to show Autumn. Normally she would feel immediate guilt for such an act, ripping down a poster. It was far too impulsive for the normal Jones. But today Prue Timberley had simply gone too far!

Jones strode down the street, expecting everyone in her way to move. Fortunately for anyone on the street, the town wasn't particularly busy, so only a few people gave her a sideways glance as she marched down the footpath. Jones was devastated to see that many of them were holding matching but smaller versions of the poster.

Jones wanted to scream, and it was made worse as she spotted even more posters in the windows of various shops and offices on the way. Jones could only imagine what she looked like. She felt as though flames were flickering from her ears and steam was rising from the top of her head. Jones wouldn't have been surprised if the sound of a train whistle suddenly burst from her mouth.

Rushing past Hugo's, Jones was pleased to see his windows were completely poster free. She hoped it was because Hugo was defending her, and not merely because it would ruin the aesthetic of his bar.

Jones fumbled with the key before finally unlocking the door and bursting into The Memory Bank.

"Autumn!" she shouted. "Autumn, are you there?"

With a whoosh, Autumn appeared in front of Jones., wearing a red and white polka dot dress. "What is it? What's wrong?" Her eyes were bulging in panic.

"Prue! That's what's wrong!" Jones ranted, shaking the fist that clutched the balled-up poster in front of her before storming towards the counter.

"Prue! Prue Timberley?" Autumn floated briskly after her.

"Yes! Of course Prue Timberley! She's put these all over town," said Jones, as she unwrapped the poster and violently smoothed it out on The Memory Bank counter.

Autumn peered down at the papers and gasped. Looking at Jones, mouth gaping, Autumn was speechless.

"I know," said Jones. "Who does she think she is?" She started pacing back and forth in front of the counter, finding it impossible to stand still, not knowing how to contain her anger. Anyone else might have flung every item on the retail tables to the floor, but fortunately, Jones resisted this urge.

"I don't understand what exactly she's trying to achieve?" said Autumn, still staring intently at the poster, as though trying to decode some hidden message.

"To take The Bank from us of course," said Jones, rolling her eyes and slamming her palms on the counter. "She has crossed the line this time!"

"Yes," said Autumn. "I know that. But exactly how does she think this…this…this poster campaign is going to achieve that? Does she think you'll see it and think 'oh yes a community market is a much better idea than The Memory Bank? Let's sell!' It's ridiculous."

Jones couldn't help but laugh and then groan in frustration. "I think she's trying to get the community on her side and put pressure on me. She may even encourage the community to boycott so that we simply can't continue trading." Jones spun around and leant against the counter. She ran her hands through her hair, before putting her face in her hands and taking a long, deep breath.

"I certainly wouldn't put it past her," said Autumn. She was now floating in the air, rising much higher than Jones had seen her do previously. It was as though she was being filled with anger like the flames of a hot air balloon. "But surely everyone will see through her. I mean is she the type of person they want running half the town?"

"I think she's the type of person who's already running half the town, and she is desperate to get her hands on the other half." Jones turned back to the poster and started taking a closer look.

"All the more reason to give her no opportunity to get her hands on The Memory Bank." Autumn flew rapidly across the room and lowered herself in front of Jones. She crossed her forearms in front of her, fists clenched as though shielding herself from Prue's advances. "We must defend The Bank!"

Jones smiled, jokingly copying Autumn, before sighing and saying "So, what exactly are we supposed to do?"

Autumn shrugged and went gliding through the room, swishing her arms through all the items on the display tables, as though attempting to discover some physical powers she could use to help Jones. Before Autumn could answer there was a loud knock at the door. Jones glanced at her watch and saw that it was still too early for customers.

"Shall I just ignore it?" asked Jones. Autumn smiled at her, floated over to the window near the door and pushed her head through the glass. Quickly, she popped back in and said, "It's Jamie!"

"What is he doing here so early?" Jones frowned. What with Clancy and Prue, and the fact that she couldn't forget Jamie was also on the police suspect list, she didn't quite know if she could handle facing him today.

"I have no idea," said Autumn. "But perhaps we could get some more information out of him about Clancy. Go on, open the door."

"I'd rather not," said Jones, rolling her head back, eyes to the ceiling.

"Oh just do it!" Autumn leant her ghostly figure against the door frame.

Jones huffed and reluctantly made her way to the door.

"Hi Jamie, we're not quite open yet," said Jones, attempting to deter him from entering.

"Good, good," said Jamie. He manoeuvred himself past Jones and into The Memory Bank.

Jones swung her arm back as he entered in mock graciousness, rolling her eyes at Autumn.

"I'm glad no one else is here," said Jamie. "I haven't been able to stop thinking about our conversation the other night. I was worried perhaps I had said the wrong thing."

"What do you mean?" asked Jones.

"Well, I realise that I may have inadvertently accused Clancy of murder," Jamie shrugged, ending with a hesitant chuckle.

"Inadvertently," said Jones. "I think you *clearly* accused him of murder." Jones tilted her head and narrowed her eyes.

"Yes, yes," said Jamie. "I think you may be right. But look, I had no intention of doing so. I don't even really believe Autumn was murdered. I think the police did get it right and it was an accident. Those steps are rather steep." Jamie casually picked up a notebook, flicked the pages, and put it right back down.

"But if you thought Autumn's death was an accident, why did you suggest to me that Clancy may have had something to do with it?"

"Oh, it wasn't like that Jones," Jamie turned to face her, a slight smile on his face. "It's just, you were talking about the *possibility* of Prue having something to do with it, and I was just joining in. If we were tossing around the idea that Autumn's death was murder, then I just thought Clancy was the most likely person. But I didn't mean to suggest he killed her. Her death was an accident, plain and simple." He shook his head as though the whole idea of Autumn's death being anything other than an accident was absurd.

"Well," said Jones. "I'm not so sure about that."

"You're not?" said Jamie, his eyebrows narrowing. "What makes you say that?"

"Look, let's just call it a gut feeling," Jones shrugged, and walked back to the counter. She was hoping Jamie was finished and would be leaving shortly. She wanted to sit down and take a breather before customers started arriving.

"Ok, ok," said Jamie "Well, I wouldn't know anything about that. I suppose if you think you need to consider it, well, that's your prerogative. I just came here to let you know that I was probably out of line the other night, and to ignore everything I said!" Jamie said this with a flourish of his arm and then laughed.

"Sure," said Jones, smiling. "Well, thanks for coming by."

"Look, while I'm here," said Jamie, reaching for the satchel he had over his shoulder. He pulled out a brochure and handed it to Jones. It was one of Prue's flyers, turned into a multiple-page brochure.

"Seriously? You're giving me this," Jones said, waving it at Jamie.

"Yes, yes I am," Jamie put his palms up, pretending to block the waving brochure. "But I'm only giving it to you because I have a plan."

"A plan?" Jones pulled her head back, very confused. She wondered how he could have a plan when the posters had only gone up overnight.

"Of course. A plan. I think Prue is a complete piece of work and has no right at all to be distributing these around the region."

"The region?" asked Jones. "She's distributing these further than just Lilly Pilly Creek?"

"Yes," said Jamie. "She's mailed these out to numerous potential investor types, including me."

"You're a potential investor type?" Jones asked. Jones realised she didn't know all that much about what Jamie did. All she knew was he had something to do with real estate or building or something in that field.

"Of course," said Jamie. "I am a property investor. You know that." Jones realised she did not know that but wasn't going to admit it to Jamie. "But there's no way I'd get into bed with Prue."

Jones raised her eyebrows. "Oh, wouldn't you?"

"What are you implying?" Jamie asked with a slight smile on his face.

"Well," said Jones. "I suppose you could do worse."

"I promise you, Jones, I am neither getting into bed with Prue literally nor figuratively. No, instead I want to get in bed with you!"

Jones heard Autumn blurt out "What?" at the exact time Jones burst into laughter.

"Stop it, stop it!" Jamie said, laughing also. "Stop it, Jones. This is too much. You know I didn't mean it like that. Stop twisting my words."

"Alright," said Jones, still grinning. "Let's get rid of the bed comparison. Why don't you tell me what you want to talk about."

Jamie took a deep breath, forcing himself to stop laughing. "Jones," he finally said. "Instead of allowing Prue to force your hand and take over The Memory Bank, why don't you allow me to invest in The Memory Bank, and finally fully realise the vision your Dad and Autumn had."

"Their vision?" Jones desperately wanted to glance at Autumn to see if she knew what he was talking about. "Did Dad and Autumn have a vision?"

"Autumn used to talk to me about it a lot," said Jamie. "She said they wanted to turn The Memory Bank into a full archival level storage facility, as well as expanding into things like digital printing and publishing."

"Really?" said Jones. "Autumn never said anything to me." Jones let her eyes move sideways quickly, seeking out Autumn, but she was still well out of her eye line.

"Well, I mean it was all just dreams," said Jamie. "But I know Autumn had a real passion for publishing and wanted to help people take all the memories they have stored here and turn them into actual memories. She also wanted to help people create digital spaces so your clients could share their memories with friends and family, and ensure they were kept available forever."

"I mean it sounds amazing," said Jones. "It's just this is all news to me. I haven't even considered the possibility of getting investment to do something like that. I'm not even sure what to think right now."

"I know," said Jamie. "It's a lot, and I know it's hard when it comes to Autumn." Jamie reached into his satchel and pulled out a bound document. "I'll give you this, and perhaps when you have time, take a look, and you can let me know what you think."

Jones took it. 'Proposal for Jones Eldershaw from Royce Holdings Pty Ltd.'

"Ok, well I suppose I'll take a look when I get the chance," she said. "But Jamie, you know I can't promise anything. It's a little too soon for me to be making any big decisions."

"I understand Jones. It's not a problem. I just wanted to give you some options beyond the whirling dervish that is Prue Timberley. If you get a chance to look at it, great," said Jamie. "Well, I'll be off. And Jones," he said.

"Yes?"

"Don't let Prue get to you. Let her have her fun, but she has no power over you you know. I find it can be fun to laugh at people like her and find the humour in their antics," he smiled. "It drives people like her crazy."

"Thanks, Jamie," said Jones, trying to smile, but for some reason, she didn't feel at all happy. "I'll try."

She watched him walk away, feeling suddenly very tired and in need of a long nap or another very strong coffee. So much had happened in less than forty-eight hours, Jones thought her head might explode.

"Did you plan to turn The Bank into some big publishing house?" Jones turned to locate Autumn, once she had given Jamie time to close the door and walk away. Autumn appeared, walking out from between the stacks.

"I have no recollection of this whatsoever," said Autumn. "But I don't suppose that doesn't mean it isn't true? I mean it is quite a good idea, even if I do say so myself." She smiled, flicking her hair for effect.

"But you remember a lot of things," said Jones. "And you remember so much about The Bank. It seems strange that you would forget about a dream, a passion, that you felt so strongly about."

"It doesn't make a huge amount of sense," Autumn agreed, closing her eyes as though trying to find the memories she was missing.

Another knock sounded on the door and Jones glanced at the clock.

"Oh," she said. "It's past opening time," and dashed to the door.

CHAPTER 14

The day was steady, not busy, but there were enough customers that it was a good few hours before Autumn and Jones could talk more about Prue and Jamie and Clancy, and attempt to make sense of the last few days.

"What's still bothering me," whispered Autumn as soon as she was able to get Jones alone. "Is that I am sure that we broke up."

"You are?" Jones sat down at one of the tables looking out to the rear garden. She realised she needed to work on getting some chairs and tables out there, and give the garden a bit of a tidy-up. It was a lovely location, but it had been a little let go.

"Yes," said Autumn, sitting, or rather floating, on the chair opposite Jones. "Every time I see him, I just know it ended badly. I mean, we were never that great a couple to start with."

"Really?" said Jones. "I always thought you were both very happy, at least from what I saw."

"I suppose we were happy," said Autumn, closing her eyes, as though trying to remember. "But we never had a future. Both of us were too stubborn and too selfish. We were both living our lives for ourselves, and at the start, a lot of that coincided with having a great time together. But I always knew it would end."

"Did Jamie know that?" Jones looked at her sister, feeling sad that she never knew that Autumn and Jamie weren't happy. "Perhaps you never actually told him you wanted to break up?

"I assume he knew. At least I assume he knew we weren't happy. I mean I can't remember a conversation about it, but I just feel things had petered out, and taken their course. And then, you know, I died."

"Yes," said Jones. "I know."

Normally that would have caused Jones to giggle, but today, it just caused her to wonder, what if? What if Autumn was still alive? What future would she be planning? Perhaps she had broken up with Jamie, and if so, was there another man she was destined to be with, but it had been suddenly snuffed out?

Atlas arrived mid-morning to his work on the archiving. "Jones, Prue Timberley, well, she can just...."

"Don't say it Atlas!" said Jones, tilting her head with a smile as she made her way over to the counter. "But I know exactly what you mean."

"Well," said Atlas, shrugging, a sly smile on his face. "I'll get on with the archiving then shall I?"

"That would be amazing," said Jones. Suddenly, she heard Autumn calling.

"Tell him to keep an eye out for anything on Clancy!"

Autumn's voice was so loud Jones nearly gave the game away. Fortunately, she pulled herself together and passed the message on to Atlas.

"Clancy?"

"Yes please," said Jones. "Clancy Tupper. He used to work here when my father was at The Bank."

"Anything in particular?" asked Atlas

"No," said Jones. "Just call me over if you discover anything."

"Sure thing!" Atlas seemed to appreciate being given a mysterious mission and strode confidently over to his pile of ledgers to get started.

"Meanwhile," said Autumn, who had snuck up right beside Jones.

"Shh!" said Jones. "You almost gave me a heart attack just then."

"Sorry, sorry," said Autumn. "I do often forget that no one else can hear or see me."

"Well, please try harder," said Jones. "It's difficult to pretend you're not here when you're spooking me all the time."

"Meanwhile," Autumn tried again. "I'm still thinking about what Jamie said, and I just cannot remember any sort of grand dream for The Memory Bank."

Jones walked towards the back of The Bank, checking on the private rooms and the lockboxes, to make sure everything was in order. Autumn followed.

"The thing is, I wouldn't put it past me to have some big, glorious goal," Autumn continued. "But I feel it was more to do with events and entertaining. I can picture art exhibitions and wine tastings. Not digital publishing. That sounds nothing like me."

Jones pushed in a chair at one of the tables and pulled the door closed. She then made her way into the lockbox room, admiring the brass numbers soldered onto each locked door.

"That's what I was thinking," said Jones. "I just can't picture you on a computer setting up books for publication."

The pair of them laughed at this. "So why would Jamie say such a thing?" said Autumn.

"It does seem a little strange," said Jones. "I hate to say it, but it seems he has an ulterior motive."

"Almost as though he was in bed with-"

"Prue Timberley!" exclaimed Autumn, but instead of looking at Jones, she was facing in the opposite direction, out into The Memory Bank. "I can't believe she has the nerve to walk in here!"

CHAPTER 15

"You've got to be joking!" Jones strode out of the lockbox room towards the front entrance. Prue Timberley was strolling into The Memory Bank as though she already owned the place.

"The absolute audacity of the woman!" cried Autumn. "Make sure you give her a piece of your mind."

"Jones!" Prue called at the top of her voice. "Jones, are you here?"

Jones desperately wanted to ignore her, but she also didn't want to leave Atlas to deal with the vile woman.

"Over here!" Jones called in an overtly happy voice as she made her way into the retail space. She didn't know why, but she rolled her shoulders back and strode confidently towards Prue, attempting to appear as though she was having an amazing day, with not a care in the world.

"Jones, there you are!" said Prue. "So, what do you think? Isn't it amazing!" Prue was shaking a handful of the posters in the air, beaming.

"What? What's amazing?" Jones wasn't quite sure what her goal was, except to annoy Prue. She knew exactly what Prue thought was amazing.

"The designs! Surely you've seen them!" Prue walked right up to Jones and shoved the posters at her.

"Oh, your little posters," said Jones. "I've not had a chance to look at them. I've been too busy with customers. It's been non-stop today."

Jones tried to avoid Autumn's eyes, knowing she would be making some sort of ridiculous face behind Prue.

"Well the whole town is talking about it," said Prue. "They are *begging* me to open the market as soon as possible."

"Market?" said Jones. "Where are you planning to open that?" Jones was sure she could see a vein starting to pulse on Prue's forehead.

"Why here of course! You really didn't look at the posters, did you?" Prue's face looked genuinely shocked.

"Here? How would you hold a market here?" Jones waved her arm around as dramatically as possible. "There's no room."

"Well of course all of this would have been moved out. It won't be The Memory Bank any more." Prue spoke the sentence at a slightly slower pace, almost as though she was speaking to a toddler.

"Prue, what are you talking about?" Jones had to admit, she was thoroughly enjoying herself. She could almost picture Prue's eyes popping out of her head in exasperation. Jones had to try very hard not to crack a smile.

"Oh Jones, Autumn would have loved this," said Prue. "Here, take a look." Jones immediately stiffened. Her manipulation radar was turned on high.

"What would *my sister* have loved?" Jones put her hands on her hips and arched her eyebrows.

"The community market of course. We talked about doing something similar many times," said Prue.

"We did not!" Jones heard Autumn call out. "Why is everyone lying today!"

"Oh you did, did you? It's the first I've heard of it."

"Well, I know the two of you weren't very close, you know, in the last few years. So, it's not surprising she didn't mention it."

Jones could feel her face turn red. She wouldn't be surprised if it was verging on violet. Prue Timberley was one of the most self-centred people she had ever met. Playing dumb had been fun for a moment, but now she was bringing her sister into the conversation and saying hurtful things without a thought.

"Are you telling me that Autumn was considering selling The Memory Bank, to you?" Jones knew her voice was a touch louder than she meant. She was desperately trying to hide the fact that Prue was riling her.

"Oh yes," said Prue. "We spoke about it many times. She could see the amazing potential for the community."

"Look Prue," said Jones. "I honestly don't know how you have the nerve to behave like this. Even if it were true, that you had discussed this crazy scheme with my sister, she is dead. Only very recently at that. And yet you feel that it is somehow appropriate to manipulate me into selling The Memory Bank to you, a legacy of my family, whilst I am still grieving and trying to work out what I'm even doing." Jones locked eyes with Prue, challenging Prue to defend her spiteful behaviour.

"Jones, you know how sorry I am about Autumn," she responded, reaching out and gently touching Jones's arm. Jones looked at the hand, unmoving, and then looked back up at Prue. "But doesn't it make this an even more perfect time for you to sell? I am willing to offer you quite a sizeable sum, and you would no longer have to worry about this," waving her arm around. "This headache."

"Prue, that is enough," said Jones. She walked up beside Prue, put her hand on Prue's back and started pushing her towards the door. "All of this is entirely inappropriate. The posters are extraordinarily insensitive, and the nerve you have attempting to persuade me to sell in the depths of my grief. Honestly, I question your integrity and compassion entirely."

"Well that's putting it a little strong, don't you think?" said Prue. She had resisted Jones's hand on her back initially, almost stumbling, but accepted that she was being guided to the main door.

"Not at all!" said Jones. "Your behaviour Prue is appalling. I expect all of the posters to be removed by the end of the day. Or I will have to take legal action. And I don't want to hear from you ever again. Never, ever, again."

Jones pushed even harder on the small of Prue's back, forcing her out the door.

"Jones," said Prue. "I think you're going to regret this."

"No," said Jones. "I am entirely confident I will not." With that, she slammed the door in Prue's face.

CHAPTER 16

Jones spun around to the sound of Atlas loudly applauding and Autumn's whoops.

"Jones! That was amazing!" said Atlas.

Jones was shaking, feeling as though she might almost collapse. But she couldn't help but smile broadly at Atlas and Autumn's reaction.

She walked behind the counter and sat on one of the stools, breathing heavily. Never in her life had Jones stood up for herself like that. Perhaps it was easier when her sister was at the centre of the drama, and not herself, but she still couldn't quite believe she had stood her ground in front of a much more experienced negotiator as Prue Timberley.

"I think I need a gin," said Jones.

"Well I can help with that," a voice came from The Memory Bank's open doorway.

Jones's head snapped up to see Hugo walking across the room.

Jones was surprised to see him but managed to respond. "I think a gin for lunch would have me falling asleep," she joked.

Hugo walked up to the counter and leant his check-shirted elbow on the top. He looked at Jones and furrowed his brow. "Jones," he said. "I just wanted you to know that I think what Prue is doing is appalling and I in no way support it."

"Thank you, Hugo," said Jones, slightly taken aback by his earnestness, her cheeks no doubt reddening. "I did notice you didn't have any posters in *your* windows."

"Absolutely not! Not to say that Prue didn't try, but I put her in her place," he grinned.

Jones spotted Autumn to the side, hands on her hips and smiling.

"So did Jones!" Atlas piped up. "You should have seen her just now!"

"I thought I heard a bit of a ruckus," said Hugo. "So you gave Prue a piece of your mind, did you?"

Jones smiled, both picturing Prue's shocked face and also Hugo's use of the worked ruckus. Who *was* this guy?

"I'm amazed I was able to hold myself together," said Jones. "I can't believe she's so persistent. She honestly believes she can get anything she wants."

"People like her often do," said Hugo. "It wouldn't be a common experience for Prue to have someone stand up to her, as you did."

"And you too," said Jones. "You told her no when the rest of the town doesn't seem to have been able to."

Hugo nodded and ran his hand through his thick brown hair. "Well listen, I'm going to sort that out."

"You are?" said Jones. She couldn't imagine how.

"If it's ok with you," said Hugo. "I was going to get the word out that you haven't agreed to Prue's plans and for everyone to remove the posters. What do you think?"

"I didn't realise you had so much power in Lilly Pilly Creek. Why wasn't I made aware?" Jones said with a cheeky grin on her face.

"It's not me, it's the magic of being a bartender," Hugo laughed.

"Can I get some of the magic?" joked Atlas.

"But seriously, I have the ear of a lot of people when I'm pouring drinks, so I'll make sure I let everyone know."

"Thank you very much, Hugo," Jones said. "But why would you do that for me?"

"Because it's the right thing to do," said Hugo. "And because I've seen the work you and your sister have put into The Memory Bank. The history you have in this town. It shouldn't be so easily dismissed by someone of the likes of Prue Timerbley."

Who was he? Someone new to the town didn't usually have such sway over the locals. Nor did they put themselves on the line, especially when they ran their own business which relied on the patronage of those locals. Jones wondered if he had perhaps had feelings for his sister. Perhaps he was doing this for her. Jones glanced up at her sister, who was staring with equal intensity back at her. She smiled.

"Well," said Jones. "I of course completely agree with you. I am doing this all for my dad and my sister. I don't know what the future holds for me, but I just cannot let The Memory Bank get into Prue's hands."

Jones looked closely at Hugo and said "I don't know if I'm going to stay here, but the more people want to snatch The Memory Bank away from me, the tighter I find myself holding on."

"You have to do what's right for you," said Hugo. "It may or may not be The Memory Bank, but at least make the decision on your terms."

Jones stared at him, wondering if she were looking at a sage or some sort of alcohol-serving monk.

"Well," he said. "I'd better be off! The lunch run will be starting and I should be there. The window has my name on it after all!" He waved as he walked out of The Memory Bank, and Jones waved back.

"O.M.G" Autumn whispered in Jones's ear, who swatted her away like a fly.

"How do you get to be so cool?" Atlas asked, staring wistfully after Hugo.

"I have absolutely no idea," said Jones. The three of them stared at the closed door for a few moments before Jones got ahold of herself, shook her head and said "right, what needs doing?"

Jones wandered off into The Memory Bank, intending to have a quiet moment with Autumn.

"Well isn't Hugo quite the knight in shining armour," grinned Autumn, dipping her shoulder.

"Oh shh," said Jones. "He just knows that Prue Timberley isn't good for Lilly Pilly Creek, just as much as we do. The more people who stand up to her, the better the outcome for everyone, including Hugo." Despite her protest, Jones felt her cheeks turn pink.

"The question is," said Autumn. "Is she so determined that she would kill for it?"

It took Jones a moment to understand what Autumn meant. "You think she may have killed you?" asked Jones.

"Yes, and I'm worried you might be next," said Autumn.

"Surely not," said Jones, almost dropping the book she had taken from a shelf in an effort to appear busy.

"Well, who knows," said Autumn. "But she does seem to feel rather strongly about making The Memory Bank her own. Perhaps I was her first victim, and nothing is going to stop her."

Jones took in what Autumn was saying but, realising customers had entered the store, she switched her focus and worked diligently for the next few hours. Jones was glad for the distraction. A few people added to their lockboxes, and a number were purchasing gifts for family and friends, which touched Jones's heart. It was lovely that people appreciated what they were selling so much that they were willing to buy for others.

As things got quieter later that afternoon, Jones felt a sickness in her stomach and went to find Autumn.

"What should we do?" As the day had gone on Autumn's words had played over in her mind. Now Jones was feeling genuinely frightened for the first time since investigating her sister's murder. Autumn was right. Prue was extraordinarily persistent and seemed to have nerves of steel. Perhaps a little murder to get what she wanted wasn't that much of a stretch for a woman like her.

"I feel a little eavesdropping is in order," Autumn was rubbing her hands in front of her. "How about you go grab a coffee?"

"Where are you going to eavesdrop?" asked Jones, who couldn't quite keep up with Autumn's thought process.

"Prue's office of course!" said Autumn. "I can only imagine her reaction after what you said to her. No doubt she's taking it out on her staff."

Jones liked the idea and was beginning to see how useful it was to have a ghost around.

"I suppose it won't hurt to leave Atlas here again," said Jones. "But what exactly do you have planned?"

"Let's just say, it would be better for us if we had a little bit of inside information on our number one adversary." Suddenly, Autumn spun around rapidly in mid-air and the next thing there she stood wearing a red trench coat and a fedora. She looked glorious and ridiculous at the same time.

Jones was gaping at her sister, flabbergasted that Autumn could pull such a move.

"Well hello there, Detective Eldershaw!" Jones said with a laugh.

"And hello to you too, Detective Eldershaw," Autumn responded. "I was working on that all night!"

Jones found this hilarious. "Well, it's an amazing party trick. Not exactly inconspicuous. And how about Private Investigators instead?"

"Let's work on it," said Autumn, and she waved for Jones to follow her.

"Atlas!" Jones called. "I'm just popping out for a coffee. Are you ok to hold the fort?"

"Absolutely! Grab a gin if you like!" Atlas laughed at his joke and turned back to the computer.

CHAPTER 17

"We totally should get a gin later," said Autumn, a smirk on her face.

"Oh, should we now?" said Jones. However, as they walked towards Prue's office, Jones realised that she would quite like to get a gin at Hugo's. Perhaps she would sit at the bar this time, and listen to Hugo as he imparted wisdom to his patrons. He might have a bit more wisdom for her as well.

Fortunately, Sybil's coffee van wasn't parked too far away from Prue's office. Autumn slid into Prue's whilst Jones continued to Sybil's. She would do her best to dawdle, chat with Sybil, and slowly wander back in the direction of Prue's office. Hopefully, that would give Autumn enough time to glide around and gather some useful information. Jones had no idea what Autumn thought she would discover. She doubted Prue was going to come right out and say she killed Autumn, or leave a secret diary open in which she confesses all. But Jones realised that since she had a ghost at her disposal it would be a waste not to attempt to utilise it. Especially when Prue had herself sunk to numerous lows today. It did appear to be a matter of life and death after all.

"Back again Jones!" said Sybil as she steamed a jug of milk for one of the three customers milling around the van. Jones looked at them to smile, but not one of them would catch her eye. They either looked at the ground or maintained a laser focus on Sybil.

"Let's just say, I needed some fresh air," said Jones. Jones rolled her eyes and Sybil nodded.

"Well, I'll be with you in a moment."

Jones was happy for the quiet moment. She leaned against the corner of the van and looked back down the street. The tree-lined Main Street and the arching wrought iron lamp posts made quite an impression when you stood back and took the time to look. Lilly Pilly Creek was a lovely town, a postcard perhaps, even when you did live here. If Jones was honest with herself, she was enjoying being back. She felt she was almost fitting in, like a puzzle piece that had some crumpled edges and was a little bent. It used to fit the puzzle perfectly. However, these days you could force it to fit, but it would never be as smooth as when the puzzle was new. Lilly Pilly Creek was familiar, and would always be the place she called home. Yet, it was different returning as an adult to the town she had grown up in. Things were the same, but so much had changed. What you thought you understood looked different, had a filter over the top, and memories and stories in the background that you weren't sure you wanted to think about.

Jones hadn't planned to stay when she returned to organise Autumn's funeral. It hadn't even crossed her mind. She knew she would have to do something about The Memory Bank and the house, but she had imagined she could simply lock the doors, take the keys, and nut all of that out sometime in the future, from the comfort of her city cottage. It wasn't until she found Autumn, her ghostly figure finally bringing a smile to Jones's face again, that she had decided to stay in Lilly Pilly Creek, at least for the short term. Yet every day she was here, the more energy she put into The Memory Bank, the more time she took to reacquaint herself with the town she had known since she was born, Jones realised she was starting to question if the city was the place she was meant to be.

As she tried to picture her future, Jones was a little surprised that Hugo's face had flickered across her mind. She barely knew him, and yet he had gone into bat for her, for The Memory Bank, when it seemed no one else would. No one else except perhaps Jamie. Possibly Hugo was doing this because of Autumn. She would need to ask Autumn if there was something there that she had yet to tell Jones. And if there was, what would that mean? Did it mean that a friendship, or more, was impossible with Hugo? Jones stood up and rubbed her hands on her pants, as though to brush away those thoughts and get back to more important things. Such as finding out who murdered her sister.

"Here you go Jones," said Sybil. She was reaching out with a nice large full milk flat white. Sybil knew her regular. Perhaps she was becoming a part of this town again after all. "Now, tell me, what is happening with Prue? She's got the whole town on edge about this ridiculous market idea."

"So you *do* think it's ridiculous?" Jones said as she swiped her card to pay.

"Absolutely!" said Sybil. "Well, no, the market itself is a great idea. Would be amazing for my business. But the idea that she thinks she can take over The Memory Bank. That's the ridiculous part. She's just trying to get her claws into every inch of Lilly Pilly Creek, and everyone has had enough."

"So why have they allowed her to put posters up all over their shops?" asked Jones, genuinely confused.

"That's just it. They're not their shops," said Sybil.

"They're not?" Jones took a long sip of her coffee and stared at Sybil.

"Nope. They're all owned by the one and only Prue Timberley."

"You're kidding me!" said Jones. "All of them? I mean I knew people said she owned half the town, but I didn't think they meant literally."

"Oh, they do. When it comes to the main street, I'd say she had some investment in nearly all of the buildings. So of course, they had to let Prue put up her posters."

"But not you," said Jones. "And not Hugo."

"No, not Hugo," said Sybil. "There is still a number who own their shops or they're owned by someone else. But if you saw a poster on a shop window, well that's one that Prue owns."

"Oh thank goodness," said Jones. "I thought the whole town hated me. That they wanted to get rid of The Memory Bank."

"Not at all Jones!" said Sybil. "Virtually everyone is behind you. We're supporting you one hundred per cent." Today Frank the cat was prowling around outside the coffee van. He decided he needed a good rub against Jones's legs, and she instinctively bent to give him a quick pat which was a first. She felt so relieved by what Sybil had told her. At least something had been achieved on her fake coffee trip.

"Well, I gave Prue a serving this morning," said Jones, glancing up cautiously to see Sybil's reaction.

"Did you?" Sybil laughed, slapping her hand on the coffee van's counter. "I would have loved to have been a fly on the wall!"

Jones smiled and took a big sip of coffee. "It was pretty good," she said, grinning.

The irony of it was that Autumn was doing just that right now. A human-sized, ghost-shaped fly on the wall of Prue's office. She couldn't wait to hear what Autumn would tell her.

"Thanks, Sybil. I'm very glad I stopped by. I feel so much better." Jones saw others were milling behind her, not wanting to interrupt, and thought it best she move on.

"Any time Jones," Sybil said, a serious tone to her voice. "Whenever you're not sure of something, just come past, grab a coffee and pick my brain. You know a barista gets told a lot!"

"As much as a bartender, I imagine," Jones said before she could stop herself.

Sybil looked Jones in the eyes for a moment, a smile slowly forming, before saying "No, not quite as much as a bartender. Have a good day Jones!"

Jones felt her cheeks redden. She quickly thanked Sybil and made her way back towards Prue's office. She hoped Autumn wouldn't be too far away.

Sybil's words had made Jones no longer feel like the whole town had a target on her back. Even if Prue was persistent in her treatment of Jones, she knew the town supported her. She just wondered how willing they would be to voice their opinions if it came to the crunch. It seemed Prue wielded more power in this town than Jones had realised. If it came down to the tenant standing up to the landlord, she wondered who would win.

Jones sipped her coffee as she walked, and started thinking about the gin she was planning on savouring once they had locked up The Memory Bank. She found herself anticipating chatting with Hugo and hearing all about what the locals had told him about Prue's little poster campaign. Of the small amount she knew of him, he seemed a very interesting and wise person. And there was certainly a kindness there she hadn't seen in many of the men she had dated in the past. Not that there was an extensive list. None had held her attention long enough, not able to complete with her journalism career. At least for the last five years. After the devastating end of her previous and only, long-term relationship, Jones had committed herself to her work, never again allowing a man to separate her from her dreams.

Jones did truly love being a journalist. She didn't so much enjoy having to chase down interview subjects, organise the photographer or get copy in by the deadline. It was the research and the writing she enjoyed. The hunt for the story, the information she uncovered that no one else could. The big question she would have to answer eventually was, did she want to go back to her journalism career? And if she did, where did that leave Autumn and The Memory Bank?

Even though it appeared Jamie was stretching the truth when it came to his description of Autumn's vision for The Bank, she wondered if there was a way she could bring her love of research and writing to The Memory Bank. Could she perhaps create the publishing house Jamie mentioned? But do it in her way. Plus, she would have her sister by her side and could catch up on the time they had lost whilst Autumn was still alive.

Jones suddenly felt a pang in her stomach. She and Autumn were busy trying to solve Autumn's murder, if it even was a murder. But if they solved it, what would that mean for Autumn? It seemed logical that the only reason Autumn was still here was to reveal who killed her. Why else would she have remained on earth? But if they solved it, then didn't it make sense that Autumn no longer needed to stay? Isn't that how it worked? Find out what the ghost needed to move on. Tears pricked Jones's eyes. She didn't think she could bear to lose Autumn a second time.

CHAPTER 18

As Jones made her way past Prue's office there was no sign of
Autumn. She decided to continue to Hugo's. Jones had promised she
would have a gin. It may be a touch earlier than planned, but
hopefully, Hugo wouldn't mind her popping in.

She pushed the door and as she moved from the bright sunshine
into the moody bar, Jones immediately felt calmer. There were a few
staff setting tables, and a couple of people out on the lawn. Otherwise,
the place was quiet. It was just after four thirty, so it wasn't quite time
for the after-work influx.

Jones perched herself up on one of the brown leather bar stools,
and resting her chin in her hand, looked out through the rear windows
to the gum trees lining the creek. Hugo's was in the perfect location.
The design and layout perfectly captured the countryside behind the
Lilly Pilly main street. In the distance, cows were grazing on a hillside,
and the white chimneys of a grand old farmhouse could be seen
peeking above the pine trees that bordered it. At twilight, it may even
be possible to see some kangaroos grazing across the river. For now, a
few cockatoos, with their yellow crests, squawked around one of the
river red gums, apparently vying for the best branch. A group of pink
and grey galahs swooped past, clearly on their way to an important
meeting. Jones took an audibly loud breath and relished the moment of
peace.

"Time for that gin?"

Hugo's voice didn't startle her. She smiled before she looked across at him. He was drying a glass, in a classic bartender pose, leaning against the rear bench. Hugo had obviously found his place in this bar. It flashed across her mind that Jones still didn't know where *her* place was.

"That would be lovely." Jones reached for one of the paper straws sitting in a glass in front of her and started twiddling it. "I presume it's never too early for a gin?"

"Not after the day you've had!"

Hugo went about preparing her drink. He almost treated it like an art form, the way he held the glass, tipped the bottle and gave it a slight swirl. It was fascinating how you could turn something as mundane as pouring a drink, into a mini-performance.

"Here you are." Hugo slid a sparkling cut glass across to her. The crystal clear gin had been garnished with a slice of dried blood orange and a sprig of rosemary. She took a slow sip and enjoyed the warmth sliding down her throat.

"Delicious," said Jones, savouring the gin on her tongue.

"So," said Hugo. "How are you feeling now, after your run-in with Prue?" He leant back, finding another glass to dry.

"I'm still angry, but Sybil has helped me see things a little more clearly," she replied.

"Oh yes?" He raised his eyebrows, showing his interest in what Sybil had to say.

Jones told Hugo everything Sybil had said. About how the town was behind her but had been pressured by Prue to hang the posters.

"But Prue's not the only one who seems to want to get their hands on The Bank," said Jones.

"Oh?" said Hugo. "Who else has been in your ear?"

"It's nothing," Jones smiled. "Nothing like Prue. Just Jamie Royce. Do you know Jamie?"

"I've heard of him," said Hugo, his tone revealing nothing of his opinion of the man.

"Well, he was Autumn's boyfriend," explained Jones. "He's mentioned possibly investing in The Bank. It's all confidential of course."

"Of course," said Hugo, placing the glass down, and folding his arms across his chest. "Are you thinking about it?"

"I don't know why anyone thinks I have the capacity to consider anything more than a day ahead!" Jones laughed and took another sip of her gin.

"Jones, you need to trust your own heart. Don't be swayed by all the people in this town who are only out for themselves." Hugo had put the glass down and was now leaning on the bar in front of her.

"I think Jamie is genuinely trying to help me," said Jones. "He wants to keep Autumn's memory alive." She looked down and swirled her glass.

"If you say so," said Hugo. "But really, isn't it your job to keep Autumn's memory alive?"

"Yes," said Jones. "And my dad's memory. But it's tough. At the moment I'm just too busy trying to work out what happened to Autumn."

"What do you mean?" Hugo asked.

Jones quickly realised her mistake. "Oh, just trying to work out how she ran The Bank and how it all works." Jones hoped she covered herself. Not that she had any malicious thoughts towards Hugo, but she still didn't quite know who she could trust in this town, at least with information about Autumn's possible murder.

"I can imagine it's been very hard for you," said Hugo.

Jones nodded and took another sip. The door opened and more customers came in. Hugo went off to serve them, and Jones took a look at her watch, wondering how much longer Autumn might be. Her heart tightened when she realised that perhaps Autumn wouldn't be able to find her. She had no idea she was here.

Before she could finish her drink and rush out, the bar's door opened again and someone slid into the seat next to her.

"Atlas!" Jones was startled. She had completely forgotten that she had told him she was only just popping out. Was it five o'clock already? "Oh, sorry Atlas, as you can see, I got a little sidetracked."

"I've locked up the shop, it's all good. I just had to come and tell you something, and I thought you might be in here." He seemed to be puffing, as though he had locked up The Memory Bank as fast as he could.

"What is it Atlas? You're scaring me," said Jones.

"Oh, no, nothing to be scared about," said Atlas. "It's just, you asked me to tell you about anything I might find on Clancy Tupper."

"Yes?" Jones's back straightened. "And did you?" She quickly glanced around to see if Hugo might be listening. He was distracted by customers but realised he could probably talk and listen to their conversation at the same time. Jones decided not to worry about it. It wasn't as though she and Atlas were sitting there discussing whether Clancy had murdered Autumn. Atlas was as oblivious to this theory as Hugo was.

"Well, I don't know exactly what you're trying to find or why," said Atlas. Jones realised Atlas may be pushing to be filled in, but she ignored this for now. "But, did you know that Autumn had put out a restraining order on Clancy?"

"Autumn? Don't you mean my Dad?" Jones looked at Atlas, confusion crossing her face.

"No," said Atlas. "I mean Autumn. It was about six months ago. Just before she died."

"*Autumn* put a restraining order on Clancy? Why?" Jones was trying hard to keep her voice down but couldn't believe this new piece of information.

"I don't know. It was just a quick sentence, I'm presuming written by Autumn because it was the same handwriting as everything else in the ledger," Atlas told her. "It just said 'went to police and put a restraining order on Clancy'."

"That's it?"

"That's it," said Atlas.

"Well, thank you, Atlas. This is very interesting information indeed," said Jones.

"Should I be concerned Jones?" Atlas asked. He looked at her closely, as though trying to read her mind.

Jones hesitated for a moment. She was tossing up whether it was better to keep it a secret so as not to worry him, or tell Atlas the truth for his own safety.

"Look, I'm not sure Atlas. I don't think so," attempting to act calm and collected, although not feeling anything of the sort. "But I'm going to visit the police first thing tomorrow, and if there's something I feel you should know, I'll tell you."

"Ok, no worries," said Atlas, giving her a nod and a smile.

"On that note Atlas," said Jones. "Would you perhaps be able to open up at The Bank tomorrow?"

Altas grinned. "Of course! So, shall I hold onto the key then?"

"Yes please Atlas," said Jones. "Keep it safe." Jones knew she had another copy locked in the drawer of her father's desk at home, but the big old keys were hard to come by and difficult to copy these days.

Atlas patted his chest, indicating that the key was safely sitting in a pocket of his jacket.

"Thanks, Atlas," said Jones. "And thanks for looking after the shop today."

"No problems! Well, I need to get home. Mum has a dinner roster and it's my turn tonight!" Atlas hopped off the stool and left the bar. Jones turned to watch him and saw Autumn slide in past him.

"You've been gone a while," Jones whispered, taking another sip of her gin. "I'm sorry, you obviously had no idea where I'd gone."

"Oh that's not a problem," said Autumn. "I've worked out you give off some sort of radio signal that only I can hear. I found you easily."

"That sounds entirely weird, but ok then," said Jones. "So, what did you find out?"

"Well it was a rather boring expedition, but I do have good news," said Autumn.

"What did you hear?" Jones tried to disguise her talking by wiping her mouth and holding her glass in front of her lips. She hoped she didn't look like a crazy person.

"Well, one thing I know for sure, I certainly wouldn't want to work in that office!" said Autumn. "Everyone seemed very on edge."

"Not surprising," said Jones. Jones was trying to speak in as short sentences as possible so no one would notice she was talking to herself.

"Well, she is *desperate* to get The Bank, as we know. But it sounds like she has resigned herself to the fact that it is probably not possible."

"Probably. Hah!" Jones quickly took a large gulp of gin to hide her outburst.

"Prue has heard there's another old building that might become available. In Oakbank. An old brewery I think, so she's heading over there first thing tomorrow. She asked her assistant to do some preliminary research, so looks like that poor guy is working late tonight!"

"Well, that certainly sounds promising," said Jones. "Now," Jones took another sip of gin before continuing. "I have something to ask you."

"You do?" Autumn had propped herself up with her elbows on the bar and her hands under her chin, looking closely at Jones.

"Did you take a restraining order out on Clancy?" Jones watched her sister's reaction carefully, wondering what her memories would reveal.

"Me?" Autumn's eyes widened, and then she looked to the ceiling, trying to remember.

"Yes," said Jones. "Atlas found a note you had written in the ledger, saying you had taken out a restraining order."

"When was this?" Autumn asked.

"Well, the thing is," said Jones, positioning her hand over her mouth. "It was not long before your death. About six months ago Atlas said."

Autumn gasped. "Really? Oh, you don't think it really was Clancy, do you? You don't think Clancy was the one who killed me?"

"I'm beginning to think it may have been." said Jones."But do you remember anything? Anything at all?"

"No I don't," said Autumn. "But you know that anything that happened close to my death seems to have faded from my memory. I'd say if it's written in the ledger, and my handwriting, then it must have happened."

"Well, I'm planning to go to the police in the morning to find out," said Jones.

"Excellent," said Autumn. "I'll come with you and do some more snooping!"

Jones finished her drink and waved to Hugo with thanks. She had tried to pay earlier but he said this drink was on the house. Again. She was going to have to start paying for her drinks eventually.

Autumn and Jones walked together to The Memory Bank. Standing at the front door, Jones couldn't help but push on it just to double-check Atlas had locked it correctly. She knew he would have, and felt a little guilty she had checked, but The Memory Bank was so precious and it was her responsibility to look after it. Especially with so much interest forming around it.

"So, you'll pick me up on your way to the police station in the morning?" asked Autumn.

"Absolutely!" said Jones. "Have a good night." Jones wasn't sure if ghosts slept, so this seemed like an appropriate evening farewell.

"Night Jones," said Autumn, and she slipped through the door and into The Memory Bank.

CHAPTER 19

The air was beginning to cool as Jones made her way home. She caught the whiff of a barbecue cooking and realised she was starving. Jones tried to remember what she had stocked in the fridge and pantry, realising that a grocery shop was probably in order. It would likely be tinned soup and toast tonight.

As she walked Jones went over the day. What with Jamie's investment proposal, Prue's ridiculous demands, and the news that Autumn had put a restraining order on Clancy, it was no wonder she was feeling both wired and exhausted, all at the same time. The bright light in the day had been Hugo. Jones didn't want to get ahead of herself, and wasn't ready to consider a relationship of any sort with anyone whilst she tried to juggle her emotions around finding Autumn's killer, and her plans for The Memory Bank. Yet she couldn't help but acknowledge, when she was ready to find someone, then a man like Hugo could be just the right fit. She wondered what his story was. Why had he come to Lilly Pilly Creek? And why a bar? It would be interesting to hear how he learned the ropes, how he had the money to buy a building, and why he seemed to be happy in a small, Adelaide Hills town.

Jones felt her tummy rumble as she turned up the path to the house. As she walked she found herself imagining inviting Hugo over for tea, and if there was anything she would possibly feel comfortable cooking for him. Culinary aptitude wasn't high on her list of skills, although this was due to a lack of time more than anything. Jones pulled her keys out of her handbag and reached to unlock the door. She was shocked to discover it was already open. Jones gasped and the hairs on the back of her neck stood up.

Standing frozen, Jones attempted to listen for any noises in the house. Not hearing anything, she slowly pushed the door open. It creaked slightly, and Jones stopped again. Nothing. Peering in on either side of the door, she looked for a weapon of some sort. She had the choice of some gumboots or an umbrella. She chose the umbrella, simply because it had a handle and would put more space between herself and a potential attacker.

Tip-toeing as quietly as her boots would allow her, Jones glanced into the living room on one side and the guest bedroom on the other. It was then that she heard a slight sound ahead. A creak and a rustling noise. It was coming from her father's study.

Desperately trying to work out what to do, she contemplated sneaking up and surprising the unknown person. Suddenly, images of police television shows flashed through her mind and she pictured the visitor gunning her down in her own house. She would prefer to avoid that thank you very much, so went with her second option.

"Who's there!" she called. There was silence, and then a crash as she heard the French doors of the study slamming against the outside wall. Jones walked briskly but cautiously to the study, anticipating that whoever it was had already left. As she slowly entered the room she saw a shadow move past the window, heading to the front yard.

Jones ran back down the hall, shoving the front door open, hoping she could catch sight of who had been in her home. Unfortunately, the large bushes planted lovingly by her mother many years ago, blocked her view. Whoever it was would have been stupid to go back across the front of the house, and they didn't. They had turned right and away. Jones quickly ran down the front path but wasn't surprised to see she was too late. The intruder clearly knew their way around and knew there was a small laneway between the neighbours' houses just ahead. They were gone, and honestly, Jones had no intention of chasing them down. It was too dangerous and she was much too scared.

Jones rushed back into the house, locking the front door behind her. She then went into her father's study to survey the damage, her heart racing. What had they been doing in here? Were they hoping to find money or valuables? The first thing Jones did was to pull the french doors closed, not for a moment considering that they would be the perfect location for fingerprints. She was pleased to see that although the latch seemed to be a little bent, she was able to close and lock them. Jones then turned to survey the room. Everything seemed to be in order, except for her father's desk. Items on top had been pushed aside and the old swivel chair and been moved. What had they been doing? It was then that she remembered the key locked in her father's desk drawer. Was that it? Were they trying to get the key to The Memory Bank? Jones felt her heart pounding. She tugged at the drawer, and her stomach dropped when she realised it was unlocked. Yanking the drawer open, she was very surprised to see the key was still there. If this was what the person had been looking for, had she caught them just in time?

Jones pulled her father's desk chair towards herself and slumped into it. Should she call the police now? Was there anything they could do tonight? She decided to call them. At the very least, she was scared. She needed someone else to advise her if she did indeed need to panic.

It wasn't Sergeant Schmidt on the phone, but one of his officers. They asked her a lot of questions and then told her things would be fine until morning. There shouldn't be any rain so any footprints outside would be still there, and to not touch anything on the desk in case there were fingerprints. Jones didn't tell them that it was possibly too late. They could work that out themselves. It didn't sound like they would do much anyway, considering nothing had been taken, at least as far as Jones could see.

Jones hung up and thought about going to bed. Yet the idea of staying in the house alone made her feel sick. Instead, even though it was now quite late, she took the key to The Memory Bank, as Atlas had her copy, and decided she would stay with her sister for the night. Jones managed to prepare herself a quick and scrappy dinner, soup and toast as anticipated. She then stuffed a backpack with clothes, a blanket, and a small cushion, before heading to The Memory Bank.

CHAPTER 20

Autumn was surprised to see Jones when she arrived at The Memory Bank after dark. She was even more surprised when Jones told her what had happened.

"This is starting to get serious, isn't it?" said Autumn, looking very concerned.

"It is," said Jones, before letting out a long yawn. "But for now, I want to work out the most comfortable place to sleep. Or am I dreaming?"

"Follow me!" Autumn said.

Autumn lead Jones to one of the meeting rooms used for people accessing their lockboxes. She pointed at a bookcase.

"Behind there," said Autumn.

"What? You want me to move this?" Jones stared at her sister, unsure how a bookshelf was going to turn into a comfortable bed.

"You'll see," said Autumn smugly. "I'd help if I could, but you know, being a ghost and all, makes moving furniture a bit tricky."

Jones, in her exhausted state, pulled book after book off the shelf before even attempting to push aside the tall, solid wood shelves.

"This better be worth it," said Jones, puffing, and sweating.

"It will be!" said Autumn.

Finally, Jones had removed enough books that she could push the bookshelf safely. She was surprised to see a door hidden behind.

"Open it!" said Autumn.

Jones was sure the door would be locked and all her work would be for nothing, but she twisted the door handle back and forth a few times, and then with a hip bump, the door opened. There was a small room that Jones couldn't recall ever seeing. Inside was a well-worn but comfortable-looking couch, an old television, and, even more surprising, a vintage bar fridge and a small gas stove top. It was all covered in dust.

"What is this place?"

"I'm not sure," said Autumn. "I only discovered it recently, in my ghostly form. I've never seen it before either."

"Well, I am just very thankful for the couch, even if it is a bit musty," said Jones. "Thank you."

"Of course!" said Autumn. "It's going to be fun. Just like when we were kids!"

But if Autumn was planning to spend the night whispering and giggling she was going to be sorely disappointed. As soon as Jones had positioned her cushion on the couch, and pulled the blanket over her, she had fallen into the deep sleep of someone who knew she was in as safe a place as possible.

Autumn sat there, perched on top of the bar fridge, and enjoyed the peace of watching her sister sleep. Jones was completely unaware that Autumn spent the rest of the night watching over her.

CHAPTER 21

Jones slept soundly enough, but she woke early. The couch had been perfectly comfortable for most of the night, but by early morning her body had started to complain. Jones woke just before six o'clock, groaning as she sat up, massaging her neck. Grabbing her bag, Jones pulled out the clothes she had shoved in the night before. She couldn't help but laugh when she saw that the t-shirt she had chosen read "Life is tough but so are you" in bright rainbow colours.

Autumn floated into the room as soon as she heard her sister moving, and the two of them spent the next hour discussing the break-in and what it might mean. Their two prime suspects, Prue and Clancy, both had the motive to steal the key if that was in fact what the intruder was looking for. Prue, because she somehow believed it would lead to her taking over The Memory Bank. And Clancy, because, well, he'd done it before, so why wouldn't he still be interested in accessing the lockboxes? Perhaps their meeting the other night had stirred something up in Clancy. His compulsive desire to use the lockboxes against others for his benefit may have returned, if it had ever left.

When it got to the time Sybil's coffee van would be opening, neither of them was any closer to deciding who it could have been who had broken into the house the night before. Autumn remained at The Memory Bank, whilst Jones made a beeline for Sybil's, desperate for her morning double shot. She was pleased the van was already busy, so she didn't have to attempt a conversation with Sybil. Jones was still in shock and wasn't sure she could hold a proper conversation.

Sybil handed Jones her coffee, and an addition to her order, a fresh piece of banana bread. Jones devoured it on the walk back to The Bank.

"Should I be worried?" asked Jones, as she settled down to drink her coffee at one of The Memory Bank's customer tables. "I mean it does seem that someone is desperate to get into The Bank. Do you think whoever it is would kill me if I got in their way?"

"I think we have to consider it," said Autumn. "It is seeming almost inevitable that I was pushed down those stairs. Who's to say they wouldn't hesitate to do it to you too if you tried to stop them?

"Or Atlas," said Jones, suddenly feeling sick at the thought. "I've been leaving Atlas here by himself a lot. How could I? What if Clancy or Prue took advantage of that and forced their way in? What if they hurt Atlas, or worse!"

"Jones, I know how you're feeling," Autumn reached out, attempting to pat her sister's hand. "But nothing has happened yet. And as soon as the police station opens, you'll go to them, and tell them everything. Hopefully whoever it was has left a clue at your house, and they can be stopped before anything serious happens."

"Do you think it will be that easy? Do you think they'll go so far as to investigate the break-in, even though nothing was taken?"

"I have no idea," said Autumn. "I mean it seems like they messed up my investigation, so who knows how rigorous they are? But we know quite a bit that they don't know. It can only help."

They heard a key in the front door and froze.

"You don't think-" Jones whispered in horror, pushing herself out of her chair, picturing Clancy or Prue on the other side of the door and having the audacity to just let themselves in.

Autumn poked her head through the wall and quickly popped back in. "It's just Atlas!"

"Oh thank God," said Jones, slumping back down. "I'd completely forgotten I'd asked him to open up this morning."

Atlas walked in and exclaimed "Jones! I thought you were going to the police station this morning?"

"Oh, I will be Atlas! Sorry I didn't let you know I was here," said Jones, getting up from the table and walking over to him. "I completely forgot, after everything that happened last night."

"Last night?" Atlas said, narrowing his eyes.

Autumn whispers in Jones's ear. "Tell him. Tell him everything. You can trust him, and I think we need all the help we can get."

"Atlas, do you mind just locking the door first," said Jones. "Then I'll tell you everything."

Once the door was locked, and Atlas had joined Jones at the table, she proceeded to tell him about the break-in, Clancy's blackmailing and the restraining order, and her belief that Autumn's death may not have been an accident after all.

"What! You mean you think Clancy might have…." Atlas trailed off, mouth agape.

"Look Atlas, I don't know. And we have to remember Prue has been a nasty piece of work also," said Jones. "I don't want to go around accusing people of murder, but something suspicious is going on, and I would hate to put you in the middle of it."

"Oh Jones, I'm fine. I can take care of myself," said Atlas. "I've been taking taekwondo lessons since I was seven!" With that Atlas stood and pulled out an elaborate hand and leg movement with a final kick at the end. Jones was impressed, but not quite sure if it would be enough to stop a potential killer.

"That's amazing Atlas," said Jones. "And good to know. But honestly, I think we best close The Bank this morning, at least until I'm back from the police station. I'll feel much better if you aren't left here alone."

"But what about you Jones? I think you're the more likely target than I am. Who's going to keep you safe?"

"He has a point," said Autumn, raising her eyebrows at Jones.

"Ok Atlas," Jones signed. "How about we agree that the two of us are to be in The Bank together during opening hours, and if we can't, then we just have to lock up. What do you think?"

"Deal," said Atlas.

"Ok, so I'm heading to the police station now," said Jones. "What will you do?"

"What I want to do is go around to Clancy's and give him a piece of my mind!" Atlas pulled out a few more martial arts moves.

"Atlas!" Jones reprimanded. "We don't even know if Clancy has anything to do with it."

Atlas grinned. "I'm joking, I'm joking! I'm not that brave! Look, I should be ok in here if you lock me in, shouldn't I?"

"I don't need to lock you in," said Jones. "You can lock yourself in. But perhaps you should go across to Hugo's instead, just for now.

What if someone tries to break in here when I'm away?" Jones knew she had no hope of hiding the complete terror on her face at the idea that something could happen to The Memory Bank or anyone she cared for.

"Ok, I'll go into Hugo's if he's open," Atlas conceded. "I can sit at the front window and keep an eye on things."

"Alright," said Jones. " That sounds like a plan." She couldn't deny that was a good idea. "Then follow me out. You've got your key?"

Atlas held it up to show her.

"Good, let's lock up and see if Hugo's in," said Jones.

Autumn couldn't resist a little sing-song "Hugo, oooh" as they left The Memory Bank. Jones let Atlas walk in front of her and rolled her eyes at Autumn, silently mouthing "shut up" to her sister.

Hugo was most certainly in. Jones wondered when he ever got any sleep. And of course, he was more than happy for Atlas to sit inside, especially once Jones told him about the break-in.

"What!" said Hugo. "Who do you think it was? What were they looking for? Have you gone to the police?"

Jones pointedly looks at Atlas, attempting to convey that they needed to keep some things between just them, before responding to Hugo. "We don't have any idea. It's probably just something random, but in case it has something to do with all this mess with Prue or someone else who's unhappy with me, I'd much rather Atlas wasn't left in The Bank alone."

"Absolutely!" said Hugo. "He is safe with me."

"I'm not a child you know," said Atlas, but only half-heartedly as he got out his laptop and set himself up at a table at the front window.

"And yes, I'm heading to the police station right now and will come straight back here," said Jones.

"Are you sure you don't want someone to come with you?" asked Hugo, a look of concern on his face.

Jones smiled, remembering that Hugo and Atlas had no idea she wouldn't be going alone. "Thank you, but I'll be fine. If someone is going to try and attack me in broad daylight when I'm walking down the main street, then we've got real problems. I don't imagine anyone would dare try anything so brazen." At least she hoped not.

CHAPTER 22

Jones had to admit, she wasn't feeling quite as confident as she sounded. Despite that, she waved and smiled as she left Hugo's. Having Autumn by her side was certainly a comfort however, she couldn't help but remember that if something did happen, she was completely on her own.

When Jones arrived at the police station, Sergeant Schmidt appeared to have been waiting for her.

"So, you had a break-in last night?" his face remained as impassive as always.

"Yes," said Jones. "I called last night and spoke to someone. Do you have the details?"

"Yes, it's all here," he patted an open file on the desk. "I was just about to send Officer Partridge around to see you."

"Ah, good, thanks," said Jones. "Look, I'm not sure if they're connected, but I did have a question for you. Before all of this happened, yesterday I read in one of our ledgers that Autumn had put a restraining order out on Clancy Tupper. Is that true?"

Sergeant Schmidt narrowed his eyes and pursed his lips. "Well now, technically I can't say anything-"

"But don't you think it's possible Clancy has something to do with this!" The lack of information that she was getting from the police was starting to get her goat. "I mean if Autumn was afraid of him, then it makes sense that we should be concerned, right?" Jones let out a sigh of exasperation.

"Now Jones," said Sergeant Schmidt. "I know this is frustrating and scary. What I can tell you is that yes, there is a history between him and your family."

"My father too?" asked Jones. She thought her father hadn't gone to the police about Clancy.

"Yes, your father, *and* your sister," Sergeant Schmidt raised his eyebrows, indicating he wanted Jones to read between the lines. Jones just had no idea what those lines were.

Meanwhile, Autumn had flitted behind the desk and was doing her best to read the open file in front of Sergeant Schmidt.

"Tell him about Prue," whispered Autumn, for once remembering not to startle Jones in public.

Jones nodded slightly and said, "I'd also like to bring Prue Timberley to your attention."

"Oh? Why is that?"

"Well, you may have heard that she has a campaign to take over The Memory Bank," said Jones.

"Yes, I had heard that," said Sergeant Schmidt. Jones for a moment thought she saw a hint of a smile on his face but didn't know how to read that so ignored it.

"Well, she has been rather aggressive with me, and yes, I have witnesses," Jones added when she saw Sergeant Schmidt raise his eyebrows slightly. "I just thought it was important I mention it, just in case it may be connected to the break-in, and, ah, any other cases."

"What I can say," said the Sergeant slowly. "Is that we will be following all lines of enquiry about the break-in, and I can assure you, we won't leave any, ah, stone left unturned." He tilted his head and raised his eyebrows.

Jones nodded, making it clear she understood that he understood. "Good, good."

"Now, about the break-in," he continued. "I will need to take a statement from you. What if we do that now, and Officer Partridge takes your keys and heads on over to the house? That way we can get things moving as quickly as possible."

"Ok, sure," said Jones, reaching into her handbag. She pulled out both her normal key ring and the large key to The Memory Bank. Hesitating, she held up the big key and said "I think this is what they were looking for. I think they were looking for this key to break into The Memory Bank?"

"Really?" said Schmidt, frowning.

"They had barely disturbed anything, except some items on the desk and the chair, right near the drawer this key was in," Jones told him. "The drawer was unlocked, which I'm sure it hadn't been previously. I think I disturbed them at exactly the right moment."

"Interesting," said Sergeant Schmidt. He looked like he was about to say more, but the front door suddenly burst open.

"Schmidt! When are you going to do something about bloody Jamie Royce!" A scruffy man, who appeared to have just gotten off a tractor, barged in and slammed his fist down on the counter.

"Come on Bronte, we can talk about this another time," said Sergeant Schmidt in an even tone.

"That's what you always say!" the man shouted. "But I tell you, we've had enough of it. He's stirring up trouble again, just like last time. He's already caused enough misery in this town. He's a swindler, and he's trying to take our money again. Can't you do anything about it?"

Jones turned to stare at the man. Jamie, a swindler? What was he talking about? She looked at Autumn whose eyes were wide open.

"Look Bronte, can you come back later, I've got to take a statement," he said, indicating Jones standing in front of him.

"Take *my* statement!" said Bronte. "And I can round up a few more if you'd like! You've got to do something about him."

"Bronte, unfortunately, he hasn't technically broken any laws. The only thing I can do is encourage people not to invest with him. But it's not a police matter unless theft or fraud can be proven."

"Isn't the lack of any apartment building enough evidence for you!" The man pulled his cap off and ran his hands through his black hair.

"Bronte, enough!" Schmidt moved out from behind the counter. "You can make an appointment to come back another day, but I have urgent business now."

Sergeant Schmidt pushed Bronte out the door and closed it firmly.

"What was that about?" said Jones, her eyes no doubt bulging out of her head. Autumn was at Jones's side, waiting to hear what the Sergeant had to say.

"Oh nothing, Bronte just has a bee in his bonnet." Sergeant Schmidt walked back behind the counter, before flipping the break-in case file closed.

"Was he talking about Jamie Royce?" asked Jones. "You know he was Autumn's boyfriend right?"

"Yes, yes," said Sergeant. "I knew about that. It doesn't mean I can tell you anything. Not that there's much to tell. Just a few people decided to trust him and invest in his company without getting proper financial advice. The investment fell through and they're convinced Jamie pulled the wool over their eyes. I keep trying to tell them that no investment is guaranteed and that it's their own fault. Nothing the police can do about it." This was the most Jones had ever heard the Sergeant say in one go, so it was clear the whole thing had him a bit riled up. This, coupled with Jones's break-in, probably wasn't the best start to his day.

"Yes well, I suppose that's true," said Jones.

Jones glanced back out the door, wondering if perhaps Jamie didn't have Autumn's legacy in his mind at all and if he perhaps had his own plans for The Memory Bank.

Before Jones got a chance to voice these concerns to Autumn, Sergeant Schmidt lead her into an interview room and took her statement.

CHAPTER 23

All during her statement, Jones could see Autumn pacing around the room. She was anxious and desperate to talk about Jamie. Autumn even let out a few "I can't believe-" and "What if-" which Jones did her best to completely ignore. As soon as Jones was finished and stepped out of the Station, she could see Autumn was about to open her mouth and get straight into it. Jones put her hand up to stop her.

"First, coffee," she said and began striding toward's Sybil's coffee van.

For a minor break-in that was likely never to be solved, Sergeant Schmidt certainly had a lot of questions to ask. A lot of detailed questions. Jones could feel a headache pricking behind her eyes and hoped that coffee might stop it in its tracks.

Sybil had spotted Jones walking up and was just pouring steamed milk into a bright pink and yellow paper cup when Jones got to the van..

"Back again already, Jones," said Sybil, grinning underneath a broad straw hat decorated with sunflowers.

Jones quickly glanced around to see if any other customers were walking up before she responded. No one other than Autumn was even close to the van. "Well Sybil, and please keep this to yourself, but I've just been giving a statement to the police."

"Oh! What happened?" Sybil appeared genuinely surprised, as though she would normally have already heard whispers of such an event occurring in her town. She handed Jones the coffee and leant forward through the van hatch, desperate to hear what Jones had to say.

"Someone attempted to break into my house last night," whispered Jones. "Well, they did break in, but it seems I interrupted them before they found what they wanted."

"And what did they want?" Sybil quickly poured herself a coffee, as though she too required a caffeine hit whilst devouring this information.

"That we don't exactly know," said Jones. She glanced at Autumn who shook her head.

Autumn then whispered "Jamie."

"But I did want to pick your brain about something," said Jones. Sybil stood and rolled her shoulders, ready to assist. "Do you know why some old farmer would have burst into the police station, ranting and raving about Jamie being a swindler and having stolen all their money?"

"That I certainly do know about," said Sybil, leaning back against the van's rear cupboards and crossing her arms. "I almost got caught in his trap as well."

"His trap?" Jones raised her eyebrows.

"I suppose it was a few months before Autumn died," Sybil told Jones. "Jamie had been approaching everyone in the town for money, claiming he was on the ground floor of a big new apartment building that was going up in the city. It was being built for international student housing, and apparently, there was guaranteed rental income once the building was built." Sybil rolled her eyes for dramatic effect and continued. "A few people put some money in, but then, after Autumn died, Jamie started putting the pressure on and saying the deadline had now moved and if everyone wanted to get in they had to put their money in now. So a rather large group of people decided to invest. After all, his girlfriend had just died, and he was grieving. The town wanted to support him, and they trusted him. The day after the funeral he got everyone to sign the papers and hand over their cheques. Then he left town and no one had heard a single thing from him until he returned last week."

Jones's mouth was wide. "Jamie was working on his investments whilst we were planning Autumn's funeral?" Jones tried to cast her mind back. She thought she had spent a lot of time with Jamie, but she did recall that he was often out of the house. Jones was probably sleeping or crying. She did a lot of that at the time. She supposed she couldn't expect Jamie not to work. The world didn't stop, just because her sister, his girlfriend, had died.

"Yes he was, and putting the thumb on a lot of people," said Sybil. "Everyone thought it was his way of coping, that he didn't mean any harm, so they overlooked his behaviour."

"So what has changed?" asked Jones. "I mean people can't expect a return on their investment yet can they? It'd be too soon."

"It's not that," said Sybil. "It's that they haven't received any proof that their investment has gone where Jamie said it has. No official receipt has been received, no updated information on the investment property, and," Sybil bent down to get closer to Jones. "That old farmer you saw in the police station, that was Bronte Schiller. He went for a little drive to Adelaide to take a look at the progress of the fancy new apartment block. Remember, this was supposedly being built for international students who were studying at one of the city universities, and was going to go up quickly. Well, the address they'd all been given wasn't near the city at all. It was well out of the city, in the middle of some industrial area, and there was no public transport to speak of. How on earth was this a good idea for international students to live here? It wouldn't be allowed."

"Seriously? Are you sure Bronte got the address right?" asked Jones. "Maybe it was just the office address."

"Perhaps. But either way, there was no office in sight, no building at all. Just empty land next to a go-cart track," said Sybil. "Bronte rang Jamie, and confronted him, but Jamie just told him it was a postal address, that the final location hadn't been decided yet, and to trust him, everything was going to plan."

"A postal address? To a block of vacant land? That does sound a bit strange," said Jones.

"Bronte thought so too," said Sybil. "So he's been rallying the troops so to speak. Your friend Wren has been trying to help them, you know, going through all the legal channels etc. But so far Jamie is proving a hard nut to crack."

"It does sound rather, unusual," said Jones. She still felt some allegiance to Jamie, as he was Autumn's boyfriend. Jones had been through a lot with Jamie in the lead-up to the funeral. He'd been such a rock for her. However, she was beginning to realise there was a lot about Jamie she didn't know. She didn't want to blindly trust everything Sybil was telling her. Of course, she would need to get Jamie's side of the story. But perhaps a little chat with Wren might be in order first.

"Thanks, Sybil," said Jones. "This has all been rather enlightening."

"Well, I'll let you know if I hear more," Sybil said. "In the meantime, I hope they find out who broke into your house!"

Jones waved, and Autumn was right at her side ready to chat.

"Jones!" Autumn said. "I remember Jamie had been pestering me to get involved in his investment. He'd been talking about it for months. He asked me too, but I said no. I didn't think it was a good idea to mix finances with a relatively new boyfriend. He wasn't happy about it and kept asking me, telling me I was missing out on the opportunity of a lifetime."

"Really?" said Jones. "How did he react when you said no?"

"I know he was annoyed, but from what I could remember he just kept trying."

"Autumn, do you feel perhaps there is more to Jamie than we realise? Like there's a lot he didn't tell you?" Jones walked into The Lilly Pilly Pantry, intending to find something more substantial than a piece of banana bread to eat.

"Possibly," said Autumn. "I certainly don't think he's telling the truth about my plans for The Bank. And I also don't think he's telling the truth about us not breaking up. I can see now that he was probably using that to play to everyone's emotions. It is sounding like I dodged a bullet there!"

"Yes, dodged a bullet but found a staircase," said Jones, before gulping at what she had said. Her eyes bulged, and she stared at Autumn. Autumn smirked and just carried on.

"It does seem more and more likely that we were broken up. I can't imagine I would have put up with him for much longer."

Jones made her way around the Pantry's shelves, trying to ignore a nagging feeling. Why was all this happening? What was she missing? Jones found some seed crackers, cheese and metwurst, plus a punnet of strawberries, and thought that seemed like a substantial enough brunch.

"Well," said Jones, as they left the Lilly Pilly Pantry and made their way back to Hugo's. "Let's forget Jamie for now. We've got more important things to sort out. Like who broke into the house, and of course, the little puzzle of who pushed you down the stairs." Jones pulled out a strawberry and ate it before speaking again. "I've at least made up my mind about one thing. I will not be letting Jamie invest in The Memory Bank. It's my Bank, our Bank, and its future is in our hands and no one else's!"

"It's future?" asked Autumn. "Does that mean you and The Memory Bank actually have a future?"

"I can't say for sure," said Jones, turning and smiling at her sister. "But it's certainly looking that way."

CHAPTER 24

Walking past Hugo's, Jones tapped on the window to let Atlas know she was heading back to The Memory Bank. He gave her a thumbs up, indicating he was following her. Jones of course would have liked to stop and chat with Hugo, but she was feeling too anxious. She just wanted to sit down with her brunch, and try and work out what on earth was going on.

When Jones and Autumn arrived at The Memory Bank, the two sisters stood outside for a moment, looking up at the gold signage on the window, the tall wooden door, and the white facade that looked glorious in the sunlight after its new paint job. They both took a deep breath, smiled, and entered.

Within seconds of entering, a customer was hot on their heels.

"Mrs Livingstone!" said Jones. "How can I help you?"

"Well, I was just wanting to set up a memory box, if that would be ok?" said the tall woman with a tight mousy bun who had made her way directly to the counter.

"Wonderful Mrs Livingstone. Let's get on to that right away," said Jones. She tried not to think about the food she was leaving in its bag on the shelf. "If you just want to take a seat at one of the tables, I'll bring some paperwork over."

Atlas had snuck in behind them and was already plopping his backpack on the counter when Jones walked up. "I'm just going to help Mrs Livingstone set up a memory box," she told Atlas.

"That's great," said Atlas. "And Jones, just so you know, I've had to start a waitlist for the Memory Boxes," said Atlas, handing her a piece of paper. "This is a list of names of people who've been in over the last few days wanting to start or update their Memory Boxes. I think you might need to start taking appointments."

"Wow!" said Jones, quickly glancing at Autumn. "I didn't realise the Memory Boxes were so popular! I thought they just sat there most of the time."

"Well, it seems that people have been waiting for you to be ready, I guess," said Atlas. "None of them wanted me to bother you with it, but they said, when you're back on your feet, they want to get the ball rolling."

"Back on my feet?" asked Jones.

"This town cares a lot about you, you know Jones," said Atlas. "They keep telling me how important The Memory Bank is, and how they want it to be here for a long time to come. So whatever makes it easier for you to consider staying, well, that's what they'll do."

"And they've been telling you all this?" asked Jones, feeling herself starting to well up.

"Yep! They sure have. People even come up to me at Hugo's or on the street. They love this place," Atlas beamed at her. "We all love this place."

Jones felt her lip quiver a little and she blinked quickly to ensure no tears tipped over. She knew the town liked The Memory Bank, but until now, she hadn't quite realised how important it was to them. The Memory Bank wasn't just about her own family and the memories she had. It was a place of memories for the whole town, and their own

didn't know about it."

"He had another key and used it to get into The Bank *after* Dad died?" Jones knew she shouldn't be surprised by another shocking revelation, but she was all the same. They just seemed to be piling up.

"Exactly! It seems his blackmailing days weren't over as he said. And I'm wondering if he had been getting into The Bank all that time, but that just before I died, I caught him."

"And putting a restraining order on him, stopping his blackmailing plans in their tracks. Well," said Jones. "That would be a very good motive for murder."

"Exactly," said Autumn. "And it would also be a good motive for breaking into our house. To steal the key back."

Jones reached into her pocket and pulled out the key she had there. "This key."

"Precisely!"

"I think it might be time we called Clancy in for a bit of a chat," said Autumn.

"Wouldn't that be dangerous?" said Jones. "Shouldn't we just pass all of this on to the police?"

"They already know about this," said Autumn. "But they're only investigating the break-in. They're not investigating my murder, at least not as far as we can gather. It's up to us! Eldershaw Sisters Private Investigators!"

"Well," said Jones, a wry smile on her face. "I think we need to do it in a public place, and with some backup."

"I think Atlas, Wren, and Hugo would do it!" said Autumn with a grin, as though she had already thought all of this through. She looked rather excited.

"Not Jamie?" asked Jones.

"Certainly not! I don't think you should have anything more to do with him. It sounds like he is well and truly a swindler and it was a good thing I broke up with him when I did! I mean, The Bank might already be in his clutches if I hadn't."

The thought made Jones shudder.

"So, we're going to confront Clancy?" asked Jones.

"I can't see we have any other choice," said Autumn.

Jones closed her eyes and took a long, deep breath. It felt as though they were really on the brink of finding out exactly what happened to Autumn. It was thrilling and scary, and, although Jones didn't want to admit it, a little too soon for her liking.

CHAPTER 25

After ensuring Mrs Livingtone's lockbox was returned to its secure home, Jones made a few quick calls to rally the troops. She then rang Clancy and asked him to meet her at The Memory Bank just before closing time. Wren and Hugo, along with Atlas, were scheduled to get there at four-thirty for a quick run down.

Atlas and Jones spent the afternoon busy serving customers. Atlas also managed to drag Jones in front of the computer so the two of them could set up a booking system online, in preparation for Jones servicing all the Memory Boxes that were on the waitlist. She was quite excited by the idea and even allowed Atlas to enable bookings up to six months into the future. She saw Autumn raise her eyebrows at this.

"Why not?" Jones shrugged later when she and Autumn met at the back of the building. "I mean I can always cancel them if I change my mind." Yet, Jones couldn't help but smile as she walked away, daring herself to imagine for a moment what life would be like in six months. She did catch herself including Autumn in that memory. Would that be the case? Would Autumn still be here in six months? In fact, would Autumn still be here tomorrow? If Clancy was the murderer, and they managed to get him to admit it tonight, what would that mean for her sister?

Jones pushed those thoughts away and didn't even bring them up later when she and Autumn, worked on planning what they would say to Clancy. If there was a chance Autumn wouldn't be here tomorrow, Jones wanted to relish every moment of today. Even if that did include

sister? Did you kill Autumn?"

"What!" Clancy's head shot up, his eyes wide. "No! Of course not! How on earth could you say such a thing?"

The way Jones's stomach clenched, the way the tears pricked in her eyes, the way her chest seemed to tighten, she knew he was telling the truth. Jones had just accused someone of murder. Someone, who it now appeared, was innocent. She felt like she might vomit on the spot.

Jones couldn't speak. She just stared wide-eyed at Clancy, somewhat mortified. She let Wren talk.

"Then how do you explain the restraining order? How do you explain the break-in last night?"

"Last night? What are you talking about?" Clancy was shaking and had tears in his eyes.

"You broke into Jones's house last night. To get the key."

"I most certainly did not!" He lifted his chin in defiance. "Look at me. How could I have broken in anywhere? I struggle to walk most places."

Jones looked at him and realised unless he was putting on a supreme act, that this was true. There was no way he could have been the person who rushed down the side of her house and out onto the street, disappearing before she reached the road. And it seemed, there was no way he would have been able to get to the top of the spiral staircase.

"But the restraining order?" said Jones.

Clancy looked down again. "I'm a stupid old man. Everything I told you the other night was true. Except for the part about never setting foot in The Bank again. I did. After your father died and Autumn took over, I realised I still had a copy of the door key. I couldn't resist. I took to sneaking in, opening the lockboxes. I was collecting information, just in case. I didn't use it against anyone this time, but I felt I needed a bit of security. I made quite a few visits. I realised that mostly I just enjoyed being in The Bank again. I didn't realise how much I missed it. I got cocky. Didn't think I would get caught. Didn't even consider the idea. Until the day Autumn returned to The Bank late and found me, sitting in one of the memory rooms, just casually going through a lockbox."

"Yes," said Autumn to Jones. "I remember now. Sitting there surrounded by papers. And his face when I found him."

"Autumn was shocked and so angry," Clancy continued. "I still don't think she knew about the blackmailing. But I realised later that she had noticed things were out of place. She knew something wasn't quite right. She went straight to the police and put that restraining order on me."

"I did," said Autumn. "I had noticed lockbox keys hung in the wrong place. I thought it was me making mistakes. I was wondering if something was wrong with me. Then it turned out it was Clancy after all."

Clancy kept talking. "Autumn was furious with me, but she remembered me when I worked for her father. She didn't want to throw me under the bus. Didn't want to cause issues. So Autumn said as long as I returned the key and promised I didn't have another copy, which I didn't, she would revoke the restraining order. But if I ever so much as spoke to her or stepped foot in The Bank, she would reinstate it, and also have me charged with breaking in. I agreed, and I never stepped foot in The Bank again. I barely leave my house these days. This is the furthest I've been in a long time. Except for that day I saw you at Sybil's. I knew you were reopening The Bank. I was pleased for you."

He looked up into Jones's eyes. "Jones, I did not kill your sister. I would never. But," he paused and looked at the table. "I wondered. I wondered if the scare I had given her perhaps contributed. Had I put her on edge, and it caused her to trip down the stairs? I don't know. But when I heard Autumn had died, I knew what I had done may have somehow contributed to it."

Tears were now dripping down Clancy's face, his nose. Jones was crying too. It was so sad. She didn't know what to say. She looked at Wren, then Atlas, and Hugo. All of them looked sad, and as though they believed him.

"Come on Clancy," said Wren. "I'll take you home."

Clancy nodded and slowly pushed himself out of the chair. He turned to walk away, but as he picked up his walking stick, he looked at Jones.

"I'm so sorry Jones."

Jones nodded and Clancy walked away, Wren guiding him slowly out the door.

"If he's lying, it was a very convincing lie," said Hugo, once Clancy and Wren had left.

"He wasn't lying," said Jones quietly.

"No, I don't think so either," said Atlas. "But if he didn't break into your house, then who did?"

"That is the big question," said Jones.

Atlas and Hugo tried to encourage Jones to join them at the Bar, but Jones said she was exhausted and just wanted to go home to bed.

"Are you sure that's safe?" asked Hugo.

"I have no idea," said Jones. "But I want to sleep in my own bed. I'll lock everything up and I'll block the French Doors. And I'll make sure my phone is right next to me ready to call the police. It's all I can do."

"Well, at least let me walk you home," said Hugo.

"I'll be fine!" said Jones.

"I insist," said Hugo. "We still don't know who broke into your house, and we don't know if your sister's killer is still around. I'll walk you home and ensure all your doors are locked."

Jones smiled and nodded. She was secretly thrilled.

Hugo and Atlas watched as Jones ensured everything at The Memory Bank was secured. Once Jones locked the front door, Atlas walked into Hugo's, and Hugo and Jones continued to her house.

"Thank you, Hugo," said Jones.

"You're welcome," he replied.

"Not just for walking me home. But for coming today. I know we don't really know each other, so I hope you didn't mind me asking you to be a part of that?"

"Not at all,' said Hugo. "I'm very pleased you thought to ask. If something had happened, if it was dangerous and I was next door, oblivious, I would have felt awful."

Hugo looked at her and smiled. She saw him reach out his hand and then pull it back quickly. Was he going to hold her hand? It almost seemed natural, as though it was something they had done before. Yet, this was the closest they had ever been, and the only time they had ever been alone together. Jones was surprised at how normal it felt.

"Clancy seems like a very sad old man," said Hugo.

"He does, doesn't he. I hope I don't have as many regrets when I'm his age," said Jones.

"I have a lot of regrets," said Hugo. "The only thing I've worked out is what we do with them. I don't want to let my regrets consume me as they've consumed Clancy."

"How are you so wise?" said Jones. They looked at each other and then glanced away.

"I don't think I'm wise," said Hugo. "I've just learnt a lot of lessons the hard way. Too many lessons."

"And now," said Jones. "Are you still learning things the hard way?"

"I don't think so," said Hugo. "Coming to Lilly Pilly Creek and opening the bar was the best thing I could have done. It's a completely fresh start for me. A new life." Hugo paused and looked at Jones. "And I've met you."

The last part was said quietly. Jones felt her cheeks go pink, but she stayed silent. Sometimes silence is the best answer.

CHAPTER 26

Hugo did as he promised. He walked Jones home, checked all the locks were secure, and even pushed her father's desk up against the french doors. They then said goodbye at the front door, and Jones locked that too.

Jones's emotions were flipping, from happiness after her walk home with Hugo, to sadness after their conversation with Clancy, and then confusion. If Clancy hadn't broken in, and if Clancy hadn't killed her sister, then who had?

Jones was too tired to think anymore. She made herself a quick dinner of pesto linguine and crusty bread, and took it out into the garden, sitting quietly at the wooden outdoor table that had been there for as long as she could remember. The evening was warm, and she heard crickets throughout the undergrowth. A rustling sound from a nearby gum tree indicated a possum was venturing out into the night.

She still couldn't believe she had accused Clancy of murder. Guilt rippled through her, but then Jones reminded herself that Clancy had broken into The Memory Bank, had taken advantage of both her father and Autumn and put The Memory Bank at great risk. Yet, he was still a frail old man. Perhaps she had gone about things in entirely the wrong way.

They were no closer to finding out who had murdered Autumn. If she had in fact been murdered. After the failure of the meeting with Clancy, Jones was doubting herself, feeling she had jumped to entirely the wrong conclusion about her sister's death. Perhaps it was time to end this manhunt before anyone else got hurt.

Before crawling into bed, as promised, Jones put her phone on charge on her bedside table, ensuring she could make a call to the police if she needed. She replayed the evening over again in her mind, and with one final smile, as she remembered what Hugo had said, Jones fell into a deep, exhausted sleep.

The next moment she heard a strange, beeping sound. Groggily sitting up, Jones couldn't place the noise until she looked at her phone. Atlas was ringing her.

"Atlas? Are you ok?" Jones asked in a panic.

"I'm fine, but I just got a strange message from The Bank."

"What?" Jones was half asleep and confused. How had The Memory Bank sent him a message?

"I'm sorry to bother you. I'd go over there and take a look but I don't have a key" said Atlas. "It's just, I'm getting a message saying someone is trying to access the computer."

"You mean you think someone is in The Bank? What time is it?" Jones sat up straighter now.

"It's just after eleven. I could be wrong. It could be a mistake. I set it up so I would be alerted if there were multiple wrong passwords entered on the computer. It's just a standard security measure. I'd forgotten about it. But I just had a text message come through. What do you think?"

"I'm sure it's nothing," said Jones, wondering if somehow Autumn had managed to channel her energy enough to access the computer. "But I'll go and take a look."

"Do you think maybe you should call the police? What if it's another break-in?" asked Atlas.

"But how would they break in? I've got both the keys. And it's almost impossible to get through that front door. It was a bank after all!" She said. "I suppose they could smash the windows at the back. But that would be unlikely, wouldn't it? A bit too risky I would have thought. No, I'll just go and check, and if it looks like there's been a break-in, I'll call the police straight away."

"Ok Jones, but please let me know what happens. If I don't hear from you in half an hour, well, I'll call the police myself."

"Alright Atlas," said Jones. "I'll go now. And thanks Atlas. Thanks for looking out for The Bank."

"You're welcome," said Atlas and he hung up.

Jones shoved a big jacket on over her pyjamas and pulled on her sneakers. She didn't feel like a walk in the middle of the night, but it was better to be safe than sorry. Ultimately, Jones was sure if something was happening at the bank, Autumn would have found a way to alert her. Jones thought the message Atlas had received was just a glitch in the computer.

Walking quickly she made her way through the town, arriving at The Memory Bank in record time. When she was halfway there she realised this was probably one of the times she could have driven her car, but shrugged it off and walked even faster. Jones went first to look around the back of The Memory Bank. It would be obvious if any windows were broken. Then she would go to the front and check if the door was secure. If it was, then everything would be ok and she would message Atlas.

As she expected, once she had looked around, Jones couldn't find anything out of the ordinary. She messaged Atlas who quickly replied to her message.

"Can you go in and check the computer? I want to know that everything is ok."

Jones was tired and just wanted to walk straight home. But she did as Atlas asked. It was the smart thing to do.

Jones unlocked the front wooden door, pushed it open and this time made sure to lock it behind her. She couldn't be too careful. As soon as she walked further into The Memory Bank, Jones realised something was unusual. She could see that the computer screen was glowing.

Jones rushed over to the computer, dropping her handbag on the counter. She glanced around, expecting to see Autumn nearby, but she couldn't find her.

On the computer screen was a flashing red message. "Too many incorrect password attempts. Computer is locked for 1 hour." Jones took a photo and sent it to Atlas. But before she could look any further, she heard a noise.

At that exact moment, Autumn flew in front of her.

"Don't make a sound!"

CHAPTER 27

"It's Jamie! Jamie is opening the lockboxes. He's looking for something."

"What-" Jones felt her stomach drop.

"Shh!! Be quiet! You've got to call the police!" Autumn was moving around the room rapidly, in a panic.

"Autumn, calm down," whispered Jones. "It's ok, I'm calling them now." Jones pulled her phone out of her handbag and dialled triple zero.

"Shhh!" Autumn hissed before Jones could press the call button. "You need to go back outside. Don't call in here or he'll hear you!" But as soon as Autumn said this, Jones's shaking hands dropped both her key and her phone on the ground. Jones froze. Autumn froze.

"Who's there?" they heard Jamie call from the memory box vault. In seconds Jones and Autumn could hear his loud strides heading in their direction.

"Jones, run! Quick!" Autumn begged.

But it was too late. Jamie had seen her.

"Jones! What a surprise." Jamie strode into the room before stopping and folding his arms.

"Ah, it's a little more surprising to see you here," Jones replied, hoping her attempt at bravado was convincing. Her legs felt like jelly.

"Well, this will make things easier, I suppose. You can just tell me where the contract is and we can pretend this never happened." Jamie was getting closer to Jones, a strange grin on his face. "But how did you know I was here?"

"The computer," Jones stuttered. What was he talking about? Contract?

"Ah, the password," Jamie nodded with understanding. "I suppose Atlas had some sort of remote alert set up. Clever little bugger," Jamie seemed to ponder Atlas's skills before he reached out and grabbed Jones's upper arm.

"Ow!" Jamie's grip was extremely strong and painful. "Jamie stop. You're scaring me."

"Oh, calm down Jones. Nothing to worry about. I just want to make sure you stay right by my side. No dashing to the police or anything."

Autumn was furious. She was flitting around but Jones could tell she had no idea what to do. Autumn tried swatting at Jamie, but it had absolutely no effect.

"What do you want Jamie?" asked Jones, a clear shake in her voice. "Why are you here? And how?"

"With my key of course!" He said, holding up a shiny silver key that looked remarkably similar to the key Jones had just dropped on the floor.

"Your key? Where did you get that?" Jones asked, her face glowering.

"It's a copy I had made," said Jamie. "You thought I was *taking* something the other night, didn't you." He had a wicked grin on his face. "But I was returning something. Returning the key I had made a copy of."

"You made a copy! Why?"

"To get into The Bank of course," Jamie rolled his eyes at Jones, tightening his grip and causing her to cry out in pain.

"But how did you know where to find it?"

"Good old Clancy," said Jamie, smirking. "Once I got him talking, Clancy told me a lot of very interesting information. Including the exact location of where your father hid his key. Once I had that, I knew I could get exactly what I wanted."

"What?" yelled Jones, not afraid to show her fury anymore. "What is it you want? What contract are you talking about?"

"The contract Autumn signed of course. Now come on, there's only one place it can be. I've looked everywhere else." Jamie yanked her arm and pulled her to the base of the spiral staircase that lead up to the tower.

"Move!" Jamie pushed her and Jones started making her way up. Autumn meanwhile had disappeared. Where had she gone? Jones was frantically hoping Atlas had somehow worked out something was wrong and was calling the police. But why would he? Jones had told him everything was ok. She was trapped with Jamie and there was no one to help her.

"What contract are you talking about?" Jones puffed as she continued up the staircase.

"The one your sister signed. In the name of The Memory Bank. She was going to invest in my apartment building."

They had reached the top of the stairs and Jamie pushed her into the room. Jones stumbled and her hip banged against the wooden table. At the same time, she thought she heard the sound of breaking glass, although she didn't have time to register exactly what it was.

"That filing cabinet. That's where it must be! I should have known. It's exactly where Autumn was standing the last time I saw her."

Jones felt a chill run down her body.

"The last time you saw Autumn was here, in this tower?" Jones turned to Jamie, her face registering the shock of what she had just heard.

"Of course it was, stupid woman. Now open that cabinet! I'm pretty sure it was the top drawer. It should be in a big yellow envelope."

"Why is this contact so important to you Jamie?" Jones was trying to delay whatever was going to happen next.

"For the money of course!" he laughed. "Your Bank is going to give me a lot of money."

"Ah, I don't think so," said Jones.

"Oh yes, it is! And your dead sister is the one who will do it."

"Surely it's impossible," said Jones. "You can't believe a contract signed by Autumn is still going to be valid."

"Of course it is! It's dated the day she died. She was still alive. And the cheque is right there with it. I only have to walk into a bank with it and they'll transfer the money straight to me."

"Not if I have anything to do with it!" said Jones.

"I guarantee you will not have a say in this. Now open the drawer!" Jamie was still gripping her upper arm, his fingers no doubt causing bruises. Jones tried to stall, hoping against hope that the police were on their way. She wanted enough time for them to get here before Jamie slipped away.

Jamie pushed her again, and Jones knew she had to open the drawer. She desperately hoped the filing cabinet was locked, but it wasn't. Everything else was so secure, so why was this unlocked? Jones realised she hadn't even looked at this filing cabinet since she had been here. It was so out of the way, she had assumed it was only here to get it out of the way, and not ever used.

She pulled it open, and indeed the drawer was empty, except for one thing. A bright yellow envelope.

"That's it!" Jamie reached in and grabbed it before Jones had a chance to snatch it.

"Thank you very much Jones for all your assistance." He wrenched her arm again, attempting to pull her back down the staircase.

Suddenly Autumn burst in. "Help is coming! Hugo is coming. Just wait a bit longer." And she flew out of the room again.

Jones barely registered what her sister said, but she did everything she could to stall Jamie.

"Why Jamie? Why are you doing this? Surely you have enough money already. All the money you've taken from everyone?"

"Oh, that was a pittance! Nothing. It helped, sure. But in this worthless town, no one believes in my vision. They won't commit. But your sister was going to. Your sister believed in me. Or so I thought." His eyes seemed to turn black as he stared at Jones.

"It's ironic really, that I'm here now, with you. The last place I saw her. The last place anyone saw her."

Jones gasped. "You!"

Autumn flew back in. "He's coming. Make some noise."

Oh I'll make some noise, thought Jones.

"You!" She yelled. "You killed my sister! It was you who pushed her down the stairs!"

"You can't prove anything. It was an accident. She fell."

"She fell by your hand!"

"I'd be very careful Jones. How sad it would be if Autumn's sister also accidentally fell down the staircase." Jamie, still gripping her arm as they stood at the top of the stairs, pushed her slightly, taking her breath away.

Autumn was standing a few steps down, a look of horror on her face.

"I remember," she said. "I remember we were arguing. He was so angry. He despised me. I told him I wasn't going to give him the contract. Told him I was going home to tear it up along with the cheque. He didn't know it was right there. I didn't want him to have it. He was so angry. He pushed me. It was him. He pushed me down the stairs."

Suddenly there was a smash of glass. The back windows.

"Jones! Are you in here?" A voice called from below. It was Hugo.

"Help!" she called before Jamie suddenly clamped his hand over her mouth.

"Keep, quiet," he hissed.

Jones ignored him. She stomped her feet and did her best to kick the noisy metal of the staircase.

"Jones!" She heard footsteps pounding up the stairs. Jones almost burst into tears, she was so relieved someone else was there. It seemed to take an eternity, but Hugo finally reached the top of the spiral staircase.

"I'd be very careful if I was you," said Jamie. "Accidents happen."

Hugo took a very slow step towards Jamie, and then in a quick motion, his forearm was up against Jamie's throat and Hugo was forcing him across the room and into the wall. Jones tumbled back with Jamie, his grip only tightening.

"Let her go," Hugo said firmly. Jamie's face was going red. Hugo was putting a lot of pressure on his throat. Jamie finally let go. It took a few more moments before Hugo released his arm. Jamie relaxed but only for a moment. Hugo had whipped one of Jamie's arms behind his back and was wrenching it painfully up.

Autumn had come right up close to Jones. She tried to put her arms around Jones. Although it was different, Jones was sure she could feel the warmth from her sister's embrace.

"Now come on," said Jamie. "This is all just a big misunderstanding."

"It didn't look like a misunderstanding to me," said Hugo. Jones looked at him. He had never looked so handsome. And more than a little scary. Jones was glad she wasn't in Jamie's position.

"Move!" And with that, Hugo shoved Jamie in front of him down the stairs.

"Jones! Are you ok?" Hugo called back.

"Yes!" Jones responded. "Just give me a minute."

She turned to Autumn. "What are we going to do?"

Autumn's face was full of rage. "I can't believe it was him! Why did I never realise how much of a sleaze bag he is!"

"I think you were perhaps working that out," said Jones. "I think that's why you never gave him the contract in the end."

Then she remembered. "The contract!" said Jones. "Where is it?"

"There," Autumn pointed to the yellow envelope that was now sitting on the top metal step.

Jones carefully grabbed it. "Evidence!" she said.

"I'm not sure we can prove anything," said Autumn. "I mean, it's not like a ghost can testify."

"We have to try," said Jones. "Maybe there is something else they can find. Come on. We'd better help Hugo."

Jones made her way down the staircase. "Slowly," her sister cautioned.

Jones put away visions of her sister tumbling down this exact staircase. She'd already pictured this when Autumn had first died. The only thing that had changed was that she now knew who had caused it.

As Jones and Autumn got to the bottom of the staircase there was a pounding on the door. After Jones unlocked it, the two police pushed their way in and saw Hugo had Jamie shoved up against a wall. It was then that Jones noticed the glass window with their gold sign was smashed.

"I did that," said Autumn, noticing where Jones was looking.

"You did?"

"It's how I got Hugo's attention," explained Autumn. "I saw him alone in the bar. It was all I could do."

"It's amazing! I didn't know you could do that. Break things I mean," said Jones.

"Neither did I." Autumn managed a small smile.

Jones looked across to the windows to the lawn, the windows she had heard shatter before Hugo arrived. "That must be how Hugo got in. I locked the door on the way in."

"Jones!" Hugo called. "The police need to speak with you."

Jones walked over, realising how little she wanted to talk to the police. How tired she was and how weak her body was feeling. But she did her best to explain that Jamie had broken in, that he had broken into her house twice to get the key, and that he was trying to get his hands on the contract. She handed it over to them.

Sergeant Schmidt looked at her. "Is there anything else?" He looked at her as if he knew.

"Yes. Jamie revealed a lot to me. I think that open case you wouldn't let me look at, and the case you said it was connected to, I think you need to chat with Jamie about that." She couldn't bring herself to say it out aloud, that Jamie had all but confessed to killing Autumn.

Sergeant Schmidt nodded. "I'll do it myself. Now, are you ok to get home? Have you got someone to stay with you?"

"I'll stay with her," said Hugo, who was walking over to them, now that the female officer had Jamie in handcuffs.

Jones was too tired to protest. He could sleep in the spare room. She knew she would feel better if he was there.

"Great. We'll secure The Memory Bank, and I'll be in touch tomorrow." Sergeant Schmidt managed a small half-smile at Jones and then turned towards Jamie. "Take him to lock up!"

Jones heard a buzzing and turned to see her phone wiggling on the floor. She picked it up only to see numerous messages from Atlas, one of the last ones saying "I'm starting to panic. I'm calling the police!"

Jones rang him straightway.

"Thanks, Atlas, thanks for calling the police."

"So you weren't ok? What happened?"

Jones did her best to explain to Atlas. He was flabbergasted.

"It was your computer alert that saved the day Atlas," Jones told him.

"I'm sure he would have been caught eventually," said Atlas.

"No Atlas, I'm not so sure about that," said Jones. "And there's more to tell you, but that can wait until tomorrow. Right now, we all need a good sleep."

Jones hung up and allowed Hugo to walk her home. Neither spoke the whole way. Once they arrived, she showed him the spare room, and then crawled into her bed, barely able to take her shoes off. Just as she was falling asleep Jones suddenly remembered Autumn. In all the confusion she hadn't even said goodbye. What if she wasn't there in the morning? Jones panicked for a few minutes, but even that wasn't enough to stop the sleep from taking over.

CHAPTER 28

Jones's sleep was restless. She pictured herself falling down those stairs, just like Autumn had. But instead of dying at the bottom, Jamie caught her and dragged her back up the stairs. This happened over and over until finally, it was Hugo that caught her and she woke up.

The memories of last night flooded her mind, and she remembered that Hugo had slept over. Glancing at her clock, she saw it was already ten o'clock. She had certainly needed a sleep-in. Last night, and all the days leading up to it, had completely drained Jones. At least now, finally, they had discovered the truth. They now knew who had murdered Autumn.

"Autumn!"

Jones leapt out of bed, dreading the thought of finding The Memory Bank empty this morning. Jones dressed hurriedly, but not before she chose the perfect t-shirt for the day. It was one Autumn had given her. "I have the best sister ever." Jones looked in the mirror, smiling despite the tears in her eyes. It had been a Christmas present and Jones had always meant to buy her one in return.

Jones had a flashback to her dream, the very last part, and then remembered that Hugo had slept over. Rushing into the kitchen, she wasn't sure whether to expect Hugo to still be there or not. Instead, she found a note on the kitchen table.

"Had to go and open the bar. Come in for breakfast. I hope you slept ok. Hugo."

Jones couldn't help but smile. Hugo had come to her rescue last night. As had Atlas. And Autumn.

The thought of Autumn this time made her stop. Jones's heart was pounding. It was as though she was hearing the news of her sister's death all over again. She had finally learnt the truth of what had happened that night. It was a relief. Yet, she was filled with worry and sadness. She fully expected to arrive at The Bank and find Autumn gone. That's how it worked with ghosts, right? You fixed what they were staying for, and then they left. Went into the light.

Knowing that she couldn't wait any longer to find out, Jones grabbed her things. Just before she left the house, she went to the fridge and took out a bottle of champagne and two glasses, popping them into a small tote bag. No matter what she found at The Memory Bank, Jones was going to drink a toast to her sister.

Jones walked slowly. She let tears stream down her face, ignoring anyone who walked past her. They were tears of sadness, relief, and confusion. For the first time since she had arrived home, she didn't know what lay in front of her. For months she had either been planning a funeral, planning The Memory Bank reopening or most recently, attempting to solve her sister's murder. Today, for the first time, she was walking into the unknown. If Autumn was no longer here, as she fully expected, then what did the future hold for her? Did it make sense for her to stay? For The Memory Bank? Possibly for Hugo? Or did it make sense for her to go back to journalism? To sell The Memory Bank to someone, but certainly not Prue, and focus on her career? Or was something completely new waiting for her?

Jones arrived at The Memory Bank. The front window was

boarded up. An orange sticker was stuck on the front door "Closed. Do Not Enter." Jones wondered if it meant her too, but she decided to ignore it. It was too important that she got in.

Taking a deep breath, she took a moment to glance up at the beautiful old building, topped by the tower that had caused so much tragedy. Pulling her key from her handbag, Jones clicked open the big wooden door.

She could still detect the smell of fresh paint lingering, but now it was mixed with the fragrance of stationery, candles and the customers that had been in and out over the last few days. The light was dim in The Memory Bank, as it always was before she flicked on the main light switch. The bare bulbs lit up and then finally, the glorious chandelier burst into light. Jones stopped and stared at it before daring to pull her eyes down to the main circular counter.

She gasped.

There, sitting on the top of the counter, long legs dangling beneath a bright red dress, was Autumn.

"Hi, Jones," she grinned.

"Hi Autumn," said Jones, beaming as she pulled something out of her tote bag. "Champagne?"

SIGN UP TO MY NEWSLETTER

Thank you so much for reading my debut novel, The Ghost of Lilly Pilly Creek. If you enjoyed the book, and would like to be notified when new books in the Lilly Pilly Creek Ghost Mysteries series are released, or other titles, I would love if you would sign up to receive my newsletter. Every now and then you may receive exclusive free bonus material, as well as my latest news or when titles go on sale. If you would like to sign up please visit my website abbielmartin.com

ABOUT THE AUTHOR

Abbie L. Martin is a South Australian author who lives with her family in a small town very similar to Lilly Pilly Creek. She has been dreaming of writing and publishing since she was a child, and when she reached her forties, finally decided to take the leap. Whilst also running a business with her husband, and juggling life with three children, Abbie loves nothing better than peace and quiet with a good book and a glass of wine, preferably an Adelaide Hills sparkling.

Made in United States
North Haven, CT
31 August 2023

40975748R00124